Wyatt's STAND

**The
Colebrook
Siblings**

NEW YORK TIMES AND USA TODAY BESTSELLING AUTHOR

KAYLEA
CROSS

Wyatt's Stand

**Copyright © 2016
by Kaylea Cross**

* * * * *

**Cover Art by
Sweet 'N Spicy Designs**

* * * * *

ISBN: 978-1537235769

Dedication

To all military working dogs and their handlers.

And to PJ, my bestest little fur buddy who is always at my side while I tap away on my laptop. Love you bunches.

Guardians Of The Night

Trust in me my friend, for I am your comrade. I will protect you with my last breath. When all others have left you and the loneliness of the night closes in, I will be at your side.

Together we will conquer all obstacles, and search out those who might wish harm to others. All I ask of you is compassion, the caring touch of your hands. It is for you that I will unselfishly give my life and spend my nights unrested. Although our days together may be marked by the passing of the seasons, know that each day at your side is my reward.

My days are measured by the coming and going of your footsteps. I anticipate them at every opening of the door. You are the voice of caring when I am ill. The voice of authority when I've done wrong.

Do not chastise me unduly for I am your right arm, the sword at your side. I attempt to do only what you bid of me. I seek only to please you and remain in your favor.

Together you and I shall experience a bond only others like us will understand. When outsiders see us together, their envy will be measured by their disdain.

I will quietly listen to you and pass no judgment,

nor will your spoken words be repeated. I will remain ever silent, ever vigilant, ever loyal. And when our time together is done and you move on in the world, remember me with kind thoughts and tales. For a time we were unbeatable; nothing passed among us undetected.

If we should meet again on another street, I will gladly take up your fight. I am a Military Working Dog and together we are guardians of the night.

Author – Unknown

Author's Note

Dear reader,

Wyatt's story was very important to me. I've wanted to write about a MWD handler for a long time and finally got my chance with his book. Military and law enforcement dogs are amazing animals, and the bonds with their handlers are incredibly strong.

And, of course, my loyal puppy dog PJ is insanely excited that he made it not only into the pages of this series, but that he made the cover of this book. There will be no living with him from now on!

Hope you enjoy this one.
Happy reading!
Kaylea Cross

Chapter ONE

Wyatt Colebrook got out of his truck and strode for the front door of his cabin like the hounds of hell were chasing him.

Because they were.

Last night's events, still fresh in his mind, had stirred up the ghosts he'd been battling so hard to exorcise for the past three years. He could run from them, but he couldn't hide. Tonight, there was no escaping them.

He pushed open his front door, the familiar scents of home washing over him. This had been his sanctuary since moving in after being released from the rehabilitation facility in D.C., but even this place couldn't ease his inner turmoil.

The one-bedroom cabin was set back from the main house on his family's property, what was left of a huge parcel of land that had been in the family since before the Civil War. It was pretty spartan compared to the main house, but Wyatt liked it that way. No frills, no clutter, everything he needed and nothing more inside six hundred square feet.

At the sound of toenails clicking on the old plank floor he looked back as Grits trotted toward him. The brown and white two-year-old Cavalier King Charles Spaniel had been dumped on him by a longtime friend a few weeks ago, much to Wyatt's consternation. He was in no position to own another dog at the moment, but he hadn't been able to say no.

Poor little guy had been rescued from a puppy mill where he'd been kept caged for most of his short life, and he'd been skittish of everything at first, especially strangers. Wyatt had spent the past three weeks doing basic training and gaining the dog's trust, so Grits would be well-adjusted and have good manners when he went to his forever family. Something Wyatt just couldn't provide for him.

Apparently sensing Wyatt's mood, Grits paused a few cautious steps away, ears down, the end of his feathery-white tail swishing hesitantly. Unsure whether he was welcome to approach Wyatt or not.

Wyatt sighed and pulled off his cowboy hat, dumped it on the kitchen table. None of this was the dog's fault. "Come on," he said to Grits, who trotted over, head lowered in submission, rear end wiggling and those big brown eyes staring up at him worshipfully.

Wyatt knew for certain he didn't deserve that look.

He bent to scratch the dog's soft, floppy brown ears in reassurance anyway. Grits didn't retreat, and Wyatt received enthusiastic kisses for his efforts. Taking on a dog was an additional burden he wasn't sure he could handle right now.

He had no steady job, just helped his dad with the farm, took care of the horses and property, working from project to project when a build or reno opportunity came up. He hated the instability, the feeling of uselessness he'd been battling ever since being wounded. Try as he might, he simply didn't feel like he fit into society anymore. He was too different. Too jaded.

Too…broken. Inside *and* out.

"You've gotta be starving," he said to Grits. Given what had happened with his brother Brody last night, they hadn't made it back in time for Grits's breakfast and Wyatt felt bad for making him go hungry.

He poured out the measured amount of food into the dog's dish and was straightening when shuffling footsteps came from out on the front porch. He closed his eyes and bit back a groan, suddenly bone weary.

God, he really didn't want to have this conversation right now. His leg ached from the additional workout at his VA appointment yesterday and the stump of what had once been his right calf was sore from rubbing in the socket of his prosthesis.

As per usual, and much to his irritation, his father tramped inside without knocking, his cane thudding heavily on the floor. Though the right side of his face drooped from the stroke he'd suffered two years ago— soon after Wyatt had been discharged from the hospital after his amputation—his old man's role as a USMC gunnery sergeant for more than two decades was still evident in his rigid posture and that laser-like stare focused on Wyatt. The one that used to send a shiver up his backbone as a kid.

"Brody called me," his father said, his speech slurred. Sarge, his retired narcotics dog, was at his heels. Grits scampered over to greet the old basset hound, who basically ignored him.

Not surprising about Brody, and Wyatt was relieved he wouldn't have to go over everything in detail with his old man. Seeing it firsthand had been more than enough and he didn't feel like rehashing it. At the moment all he wanted was some peace and quiet, although having company might help keep the ghosts at bay for a little while. "He tell you what happened?"

"Most of it, I think. He sounds okay, said the NSA is handling everything for him and the girl."

Trinity Durant. Or whatever the hell her name really was. She was some sort of government-sanctioned female assassin Brody had met a few days ago, when she'd broken into his commander's house near Quantico, looking for help. Last night she'd almost gotten Brody killed in a gun battle with two mobsters.

Every time Wyatt thought about it his insides clenched. His family had been through too much already. He'd be damned if he'd allow anything more to happen to any of them.

"It was a helluva night," was all he said.

His father eyed him for a long moment. "You all right?"

Wyatt turned away, toward the fridge. "Yeah." He'd be a lot better if he had a few shots of whiskey to dull the edge though. His PTSD had mostly been under control lately—or so he'd thought. But seeing his brother in mortal danger last night had shaken him up pretty bad, dredging up things he'd rather stay buried.

A chair scraped over the planks as his dad seated himself, apparently aiming to make himself comfortable and stay awhile. It didn't escape Wyatt's notice that he'd chosen to sit off to the left side of the table, where Wyatt could see him with his one eye. He appreciated the gesture, but in his current mood it just reminded him of how damaged he truly was. "What do you think of her?" his dad asked.

"I don't know what to think." He wanted to hate Trinity's guts for the danger she'd placed Brody in, on principle. "Brody's pretty into her, given everything he risked for her last night. And she has powerful friends. As soon as I started driving her away from the scene she

4

was already calling people to make sure Brody was cleared of any wrongdoing. If that didn't work, she was ready to expose the dirty CIA officer behind the leak on her own."

She would have been blacklisted for it, or worse. Maybe even killed. Wyatt respected her for being willing to do that. "So that has to mean she cares about Brody a lot too, to be ready to take a risk like that." Plus, Brody had told him she was worth it, so that was all Wyatt needed to know. If she was what Brody wanted, then Wyatt would have his back.

His father nodded and eyed the coffee maker. "Put on a fresh pot?"

Resigned to a long visit and fielding more questions, Wyatt dutifully turned and started pulling items from the cupboard. He could already envision how this was going to go. *I'm fine, Dad, I swear. No, I haven't been drinking. No, I'm not on any meds. The headaches don't happen that often anymore.*

With his back to his father, he said, "Brody told you to check on me, didn't he?"

"He might have."

Yeah, no *might have* about it. "I'm okay. Now that I know Brody's fine and everything's being taken care of, I'm good." Whatever he had to say to get his dad to let him be for a while.

"He said you looked pretty shaken up last night."

Wyatt swiveled to look at him with an incredulous snort. "Yeah? Well excuse me for losing my shit when I hear my brother being shot at on the other end of the phone, then track him via his phone to a deserted road in the middle of nowhere and find him and his new girlfriend crawling out of a cornfield, leaving two dead bodies behind." His pulse picked up just from saying the words.

His father didn't answer, merely watched him with that annoying calm that made Wyatt want to grind his teeth. His father had seen combat in three different wars, and knew a thing or two about post-traumatic stress. If he was haunted by his own demons, he hid it well. A trait he apparently hadn't passed onto his eldest son.

"It was good, what you did," his father said. "Family's the most important thing and we always look after our own."

Wyatt nodded once in acknowledgment and went back to making the coffee. He knew that. It had been ingrained in all of them, even before his mom got sick and died. No matter what they did or what was going on in their lives, the Colebrooks stuck together. Period.

When he'd filled two mugs he turned around to find that Grits had given up on Sarge and jumped up into his father's lap. His dad scratched the Cavalier's ears with his good hand and the dog's eyes were half-closed in bliss as Grits leaned into him.

"You're pathetic," Wyatt told Grits, who ignored him.

"Pretty cute little guy," his father commented, taking the mug Wyatt offered. "You decided yet whether you're gonna keep him?"

"No." Seemed he went back and forth about it a few times every day.

"Piper thinks he's perfect for you."

Wyatt stopped and shot him a *get real* look at the mention of his ex-high school sweetheart. "Dad." Even though they'd only dated for a few weeks and there was nothing remotely romantic between them anymore, Piper had stayed close with him and his family over the years. As far as they were all concerned, she was an honorary Colebrook.

"Well you can't just give him back now."

"Yeah, I can." He'd told Piper when she'd brought Grits over that he wasn't ready to take on a new dog—that he might never be ready again. She'd steamrolled right over all his protests in that sweet yet steel-laden way Piper had, pulling out the sympathy card by telling him Grits was a rescue dog and needed a good home.

"Who knows what kind of person he'd wind up with if you let him go?"

Wyatt had only kept Grits up to this point because he didn't have the heart to dump the dog somewhere after all the little guy had been through. "I haven't decided what to do with him yet," he said, watching Grits.

True, he was a sucker for animals, especially dogs, but he'd always owned or worked with German shepherds or Belgian Malinois. Big, strong working dogs that he trained to do important jobs like protect Marines and sniff out different kinds of explosives. Not fluffy little lapdogs that had once been bred as companions for royalty. That had all been before he'd lost Raider.

Now, everything was different. He didn't want to get attached to another dog again. It was too damn hard when they died.

"What's his story, anyway?" his dad asked, now scratching the dog's chest. Grits was licking deliriously at his father's scruffy chin, totally oblivious to how he was embarrassing himself.

"Piper said his previous owners had used him as a stud dog and kept him caged for pretty much his entire existence before he was rescued a couple months ago." God, people were such—

"Assholes," his father muttered, and Wyatt nodded in agreement.

The musical notes of Piper's special ringtone pierced the air. "Speak of the devil," Wyatt murmured, digging out his phone. "Hey," he answered. "Dad and I were just talking about you."

"Were you? All good things, I'm sure."

"Always," he deadpanned, fairly sure she was either calling to check on Grits or ask him about his VA appointment yesterday. She did it all the time, checking up on him. He didn't mind it, even liked it to a point, but she tended to mother him.

Since no one would ever replace his mother, he'd made it clear he was okay with her being his honorary sister instead. Besides, she and his sister, Charlie, loved each other. And God knew, Charlie could use the female backup in this family, having been raised with three older brothers by a former USMC gunny sergeant.

"How are things with Grits? Are you falling in love with him yet?"

"Shockingly, no."

She made a disparaging noise. "Whatever, you will. I know you too well. There's no way you can turn your back on that sweet little guy now that you've spent time with him and you know he needs you."

Wyatt scowled even though she couldn't see him. "I hate it when you say stuff like that." Damn guilt trips, tugging at the few heartstrings he had left and didn't like anyone to know about.

"It's because I know how to work you."

Yeah, she did. And knowing Piper, she was betting on him caving and keeping Grits if they spent more time together. "That why you're calling?"

"Actually, no."

Something about her tone put him on edge. "Then why, what's wrong?"

His father looked at him sharply, his coffee mug poised halfway to his lips.

"Is there a reason you ignored all my calls last night?"

"Yeah." And he didn't want to elaborate over the phone right now. He needed a few hours to decompress, then some sleep and maybe a trail ride before he felt like talking to anyone else about last night.

"Well, this was important."

He'd been a little bit busy trying to keep his brother from being killed. "Stuff came up. I'll fill you in later. So what did you keep calling me about?"

"Okay, I don't really know how to say this, so I'm just gonna say it."

Wyatt waited, tension creeping into his gut. "What?"

"The Miller house just sold this morning."

The bottom of his stomach dropped out. "*What*?" His dad was staring at him in concern now, but Wyatt didn't look at him, too blindsided by this bombshell. "What the hell do you mean, it's sold? It wasn't even up for sale yet." It couldn't have sold. Everyone in town knew he'd set his sights on the place years ago, that he'd been waiting impatiently for the widow Miller's estate to put it up for sale.

"The beneficiaries of Mrs. Miller's estate suddenly decided to list it and someone jumped on it before the news went public. The deal went through this morning. A real estate friend of mine called to tell me. That's why I'd been trying to reach you last night. I got wind that someone was interested and maybe making an offer, so I wanted to see if you could maybe make a counteroffer or something to prevent the private sale from going through. I never dreamed the deal would go through this fast, and all behind the scenes."

Wyatt dragged a hand over his face, hit with twin arrows of despair and disbelief. "Are you sure it's a done deal?"

"Yes. I'm so sorry—"

"Who's the buyer?"

9

A tense beat passed. "Wyatt, you can't—"

No. "Who is it, Piper?" His heart pounded, his fingers clenched around the phone. Panic clawed at him with icy talons. This couldn't happen. He had to stop it. Undo it somehow.

She sighed. "The name is Austen Sloan and they're over there now with the real estate agent—"

Wyatt hung up and snatched his keys from the counter.

"What's going on?" his father asked, pushing to his feet.

"Someone just bought the Miller house out from under me," he snapped, and stormed out of the cabin, ignoring Grits's pleading barks as he rushed toward his truck.

Fuck this day. Fuck *everything*.

No matter what it took, he had to get that house back. It was the only way he had left to redeem himself.

Chapter TWO

Austen couldn't stop smiling as she turned in a circle to take in the "front parlor" in her new house. Her *old* new house that needed a hell of a lot of work before it was in any kind of condition to live in.

But still. Hers, and it felt so damn good.

This was the first thing she'd had to be excited about since John died two years ago. He would want this for her, a home of her own and a fresh start. It was high time she got on with the rest of her life, and after months of searching, Sugar Hollow seemed the perfect place to do it.

Her real estate agent had just left, leaving Austen to savor the peace and satisfaction of finally having taken this huge, scary step. This day was years in the making, and now that she'd accomplished it, her emotions were mixed. Excitement, a little bit of anxiety, and of course some sadness.

Leaving her friends, her old life and all the memories that came with it had been the second hardest thing she'd ever done, but having found this grand old beauty of a house, she knew it was worth it. The house was a diamond in the rough and she intended to make it sparkle again.

Above her in the center of the eight-foot high ceiling, an antique plaster medallion framed an old light fixture that looked certain to start a fire if any electrical current flowed through its wires. Those were the least of her worries at the moment though, as outlined in detail in the inspector's report she'd received before closing the deal.

The front parlor was actually in the best shape of any room in the house. All the intricate oak woodwork alone had made her heart beat faster when she'd first come to see the place. Elaborate filigree fretwork ran the length of the arched doorway separating the living room from the entry hall, and the jambs had scrollwork carved into them. She couldn't wait to work on it.

Sure, there was a lot to be done, even in here. Apart from restoring all the woodwork, she'd have to rip out the old carpets to see if she could salvage the wood floors underneath—why did people always cover up wood floors in grand old houses like this?—and she'd need to repair some of the plaster on the walls and ceiling before she painted them. Still, this room was a fairly simple, manageable project to take on.

The rest of the house…not so much.

And lord, she didn't even want to think about what she was going to have to do in the basement/cellar. It was definitely the kind of place where slasher movies were filmed, all dark and damp, filled with cobwebs and who knew what else. A part of her was terrified that she might have bitten off more than she could chew with this house, but she pushed it aside. The deal was done, no sense second-guessing herself at this point. She'd just have to tackle the project one room at a time, not get overwhelmed.

Go big or go home, John had always told her.

Well, she'd definitely gone big here, and this *was* home now, for better or worse. She would never go back to Pennsylvania. There were too many memories there, too many daily reminders of what she'd lost. It wasn't healthy for her.

The old floorboards creaked under her feet as she walked through to the kitchen, where a mishmash of styles had all been slapped together over the decades. Thin beams of light filtered in between the boards covering the tall windows that overlooked the private backyard, illuminating the dust motes floating through the air.

Every visible surface was caked with a decade worth of dust, the paint was peeling and the electrical and plumbing systems would have to be gutted and redone from scratch. Not to mention she'd also need to put in a brand new HVAC system and new insulation in all the walls.

This grand old lady was in sad shape, and she was just the person to give it the TLC it deserved. She would restore it to its former beauty and then some—while updating it with all the modern conveniences it was lacking now. Underneath all the neglect and grime, this place had good bones. Beautiful ones.

Just standing in it filled her with excitement. She'd been lucky to come across it when she had. Apparently the family estate holding the property had been unwilling to sell it since the previous owner had died. The moment Austen had seen the place she'd fallen in love with it, and had called the agent she'd been in contact with about another property in the Sugar Hollow area.

The woman had called the lawyers responsible for the estate to inquire about its status and found out the estate was willing to sell. When they'd given a number, Austen had offered the full amount right away in cash, wanting to avoid a potential bidding war once word got out that it was for sale. An impulsive move totally unlike her, but as scary as it had been, she knew she'd made the right call. A few days later, the place was hers.

She completed her tour on the upper floor, stopping in each room to make notes of her general plan for it. Seriously, the current state of a few of the rooms scared her. What had the previous owners been thinking, decorating them like that?

The house was literally a time capsule, every decade since the 1880s represented somewhere in the decor. The 1950s-style kitchen was particularly heinous, with its peeling, checkered vinyl floors and mint green cabinets made with some kind of laminate and Formica countertops. The upstairs washroom was straight out of the 60s with a matching pink tub and sink—and not in a good way. It seemed any previous renovations to the house had been cobbled together in a half-assed way that made her inner carpenter shudder in horror.

"Don't you worry," she murmured to the house, feeling sorry for the state it was now in. "I'll fix you up and make you better than new, and I promise to keep all the pretty details that make you so special." Oh, it would be beautiful when she was done with it.

If her budget and stamina held out long enough to see it through.

At the foot of the grand wooden staircase that led from the foyer to the second floor, she paused to run a hand over the newel post. Hand carved out of oak, its fancy flourishes and scrollwork just begged to cleaned up and refinished. Painting it white would make the whole space brighter, but she wasn't sure if she could stomach covering up such lovely grained wood.

Once the boards were removed from the windows, this entire part of the house would be flooded with natural light that would make the woodwork glow. The stained glass details in the transoms and panels on either side of the front door would glow like jewels, throwing shards of colored light onto the hardwood floor she would stain and polish to a high gloss.

Stepping out onto the front porch, which was sagging a little in the center, she pried a board off one of the windows next to the door to get a better look at the glass. Not surprisingly, several panes were cracked and the casements would need to be replaced, plus the stained glass needed to be repaired and re-leaded. The plain windows she could fix herself but the stained glass bits would have to be outsourced.

She added more notes to her list and did a quick estimate. If everything came together in terms of scheduling and she could find good, reliable tradespeople to help her, she might be able to finish everything on budget in six to nine months.

Maybe. Because she was experienced enough to realize that building projects pretty much never ran according to schedule. Or on budget, for that matter. And she had only a tiny amount of wiggle room in her budget.

She turned at the sound of a vehicle coming up her driveway. A white pickup came barreling down the long, tree-bordered drive, its tires kicking up a cloud of dust behind it. A jolt of alarm shot through her when the driver screeched to a stop beside her truck, sending up more dust.

The door flew open and a man jumped out, slamming his door and storming toward her. He was big and around her age, with short dark hair and a beard.

What she could see of the right side of his face was scarred pretty badly, and she recognized the swirling pattern mixed with pockmarks as the hallmarks of a blast injury.

She'd never laid eyes on the man before but it was clear he was pissed. Austen almost backed up a step at the look on his face as he stalked toward her, a twinge of fear twisting up her spine. Except she wasn't the backing down sort.

She stepped to the front of the porch and crossed her arms over her chest, effectively barring his way to the front door as he reached the bottom of the stairs. "Can I help you?" she asked evenly.

He paused there, his jaw working for a moment. A shaft of sunlight bathed the scarred half of his face, illuminating his thick espresso-colored hair and hazel-brown eyes. "You the real estate agent?"

"No. The owner."

Shock flickered over his face for a moment. "You're Austen Sloan?"

"That's right. Is there a problem?" Because he sure as hell looked like he had one.

He crossed his arms over his chest—his very broad chest—mimicking her pose, his feet braced apart. "Yeah, there is."

She raised her eyebrows and waited, not about to be intimidated by some local asshole. Nine years as a firefighter had taught her many things, one of the most important being not to take men's shit just because she was a woman. This guy was big and built, but she wasn't exactly petite and had long ago stopped letting men use their size and attitudes to intimidate her. "And what's that?"

"There's been some kind of mistake. I've been waiting to buy this place since the former owner passed away. I was supposed to be informed by the estate's lawyers the moment this house was listed for sale, and I wasn't."

She'd been prepared for this, for someone to want to battle her for the house, because according to her agent, people had been asking the estate to sell the house for years. She just hadn't expected a confrontation so soon. "I don't know anything about that, but I assure you I bought it fair and square."

His jaw flexed and she could see the resentment burning in his eyes. "What did you pay for it?"

"None of your business."

A pause. "I'll pay you ten percent over the purchase price to sell it to me."

"No."

More jaw flexing. "Fifteen."

"No." She'd fallen in love with this house, with its charm and character and this wasn't about money. It was about restoring and building a place for her to love and make a home in. "Listen, Mr…"

"Colebrook," he answered, an impatient edge to his voice. Tension rolled off his big frame, burned in his eyes. He would have been attractive without that scowl, even with the scars.

"Colebrook," she acknowledged. "I'm sorry you didn't get a chance to bid on the house, but it's mine now. I bought it legally and I'm not interested in selling to you or anyone else. Now have a nice day." With that she spun around and headed for the front door.

"You don't understand."

She almost kept walking. She wanted to, but something about his tone stopped her. Pain.

Reaching for patience, she made herself turn around to face him. "What don't I understand? My name is on the title and the seller has my money in their bank account. Pretty sure it's my house." And it was going to cost her more than twice as much to fix it as it had to buy it.

"This house, this property, has significant…sentimental value for me."

The way he phrased it, and the way his already deep voice dropped lower when he said it, told her it cost him a lot to admit that. "It does for me too." John would have loved this place. They'd always wanted to renovate a Victorian house together. This was her chance to live her dream and honor his memory.

Those hazel eyes pinned her in place, burning with frustration and…something that tugged at her. A bleakness she recognized that came from profound loss. "I used to stay here. Have Sunday night suppers in that dining room," he said, nodding in the direction of the where the room was located. "The family who owned this place meant a lot to me. I've had my eye on it since the day Mrs. Miller died, and I've been waiting ever since for it to go up for sale."

Did he think she would change her mind because of that?

He paused, drew a deep breath and seemed to struggle to rein himself in before asking, "How much will it take to buy it off you?"

She got the sense it hadn't been easy for him to ask that. Her mind was made up though. "It's not for sale. I'm sorry." She hadn't even turned back around yet before he stopped her again.

"What are you intending to do with it?"

Again, his phrasing struck her as odd. He sounded protective of the house, as if he didn't trust her with it. Maybe he was worried she planned to bulldoze it. "I'm going to fix it up."

"And then what?"

She was losing patience now. "And then I'm going to live in it." For starters, anyway.

"You're going to stay." His tone dripped with skepticism.

Unless this town is full of assholes like you. "Yes."

He stood there for a long moment, staring at her. She held that hard gaze, refused to look away or even blink. Then he lowered his arms to his sides and his entire posture seemed etched with defeat. The desperate, almost haunted light in his eyes tugged at her, made her want to make it better somehow.

He pulled out his wallet, took out a business card and held it up. "If you ever decide to sell, will you promise to call me first? It would mean a lot," he added after a moment.

Dammit, he was making her feel freaking guilty for owning the place, when just five minutes ago she'd been basking in all her excited glory of starting this new chapter of her life. "Fine." She reached out a hand and stayed where she was, forcing him to climb the stairs to give it to her. His stride had a slight hitch to it.

When he reached the top step she caught another flash of surprise in his eyes as he realized how tall she was. A hair over six feet, putting her at about three inches shorter than him. He was a big man. Sexy, in spite of the scarring and the pissy attitude. Too bad.

He recovered quickly, stopping an arm's length away. Up close she could see the flecks of amber and green amongst the chocolate-brown in his eyes, and there was something different about his right one. It was subtle, but when she looked closely she could see it wasn't exactly the same as his left. Given the scarring on the right side of his face, maybe the right eye was a prosthetic.

He held the card out between two long fingers, and raised his eyebrows. "Promise?"

Promise what? Oh, to call him if she ever decided to sell. "I promise," she told him and took the card, careful not to touch his fingers. Dammit, he smelled good, too. Something clean and masculine, slightly citrusy.

"Thanks." He took a step back and looked past her through the front door, gazing almost longingly at the interior beyond before meeting her stare once more. "Take good care of her."

The way he said it, as if he was talking about a lover he'd just lost, made her want to hug him. She knew too well what loss felt like, and was sorry she was responsible for his. "I will."

The moment he started down the steps she went inside and closed the front door, letting out a deep breath of relief as she rested her back against it. As the sound of his truck's engine fired to life out in the driveway she read his card.

Wyatt Colebrook, contractor. Military contractor? Construction contractor?

He hadn't made the most favorable first impression, that was for sure, but she'd damn sure never forget him. Outside, his truck pulled away from the house, the sound of the engine growing fainter as he drove down the driveway.

He might be gone for now, but her gut said this situation with the house was far from over between them.

Chapter THREE

A sour sensation churned in Wyatt's stomach as he drove back home. It felt like he was in a daze. Or a bad dream. "Dammit."

He couldn't believe this had happened. How *had* it happened? Piper was a real estate agent and had promised to let him know the instant she got wind of the Miller place going up for sale. He'd been poised to pounce on it when it did.

Whatever Austen Sloan's reasons for wanting to keep the house so badly, they couldn't touch his. That house was the only remaining tangible link to a family he owed an insurmountable debt to. Wyatt had spent a lot of time there over the years, enjoying whatever Mrs. Miller had churned out of her kitchen. She'd been a fantastic cook, and a loving, doting grandmother to her only grandchild.

Taylor.

Just thinking about him made Wyatt's throat thicken and his heart pound. He'd grown up with Taylor, gone to school with him, played varsity football with him in high school. They'd enlisted together, gone to boot camp at Parris Island together. Then they were deployed together on that last tour in Afghanistan.

Taylor wasn't blood but Wyatt had considered him a brother nonetheless, every bit as much a brother to him as Brody and Easton were. And Wyatt had gotten him killed.

He swallowed hard, clenched his fingers around the steering wheel. The worst part was knowing he'd screwed up. Out on patrol during that early morning op, he'd missed the signals of a buried IED that had taken out the entire squad, including Wyatt's beloved and brave military dog, Raider.

His gaze strayed to the camo-patterned training collar hanging from the rearview mirror. God, he missed his canine partner and fellow Marines. He pulled in a deep breath, tried to shake the memories away, but couldn't. It was his fault. He'd screwed up, and everyone had died but him.

Surviving was his punishment. And every goddamn day, he had to deal with that.

When old Mrs. Miller had passed away over a year ago, he'd vowed to himself he would buy the house and fix it up, do something to honor her and Taylor's memory. Maybe turn it into a home for disabled veterans.

Now that chance was gone.

Stopping for a red light in the middle of Sugar Hollow's "downtown", he saw Piper's red car on the right at the intersection. She stuck her hand out her window and waved him down frantically.

The light turned green. He raised a hand in acknowledgment and kept driving. She swung her car around and he knew she was going to follow him all the way back to his place.

He wasn't in the mood for company at the moment, but he did want to know what the hell had happened so maybe it was best they talked now. He didn't want an audience for what would likely be a heated conversation, so if she wanted to talk, they'd have to do it at his place.

He drove down Main Street, past tidy and brightly-painted Victorian shops, restaurants and B&Bs, the architecture so like the Miller place that the sight twisted the knife currently buried under his ribs. Two miles outside of town he turned left and headed out toward the fertile farmland in the heart of the Shenandoah Valley. Normally the rolling green hills and pastureland and the sight of his family home coming into view filled him with peace.

Today, it made him feel like a five-hundred-pound boulder was sitting on his chest.

Initially, after the amputation and being released from the long term rehab facility, he'd moved back here and into the cabin to get himself back on his feet—har har—and then stayed on after his father had suffered the stroke.

As the eldest, he saw it as his job to help his dad out, lend a hand to maintain the large property and take care of the horses along with their hired help. He'd told his siblings from day one that he wanted that responsibility, and he didn't regret it.

All four of them were involved with their father's care to some extent, but Wyatt bore the brunt of it and he wanted to shoulder that weight. It had given him a purpose while he struggled to adapt to his new reality as an amputee, and his siblings were all able-bodied and busy with their own careers. His father had raised horses and built homes since Wyatt was in his teens. The stroke had left him unable to work, so Wyatt had stepped in to keep the contracting business running, although on a smaller scale on the side.

While juggling all of that, he'd been saving up to buy the Miller place, taking on reno jobs with the crew of fellow wounded vets he'd put together from here in the Valley and surrounding area. He'd promised them full time work for at least six months when he finally bought the Miller place. Now he'd let them all down too.

The two-story, pale yellow farmhouse glowed in the morning sunlight as he pulled up in front of it. His dad was sitting on the front of the wrap-around porch with Grits and Sarge.

Wyatt loved this house, this land, yet part of him felt suffocated here. Every day he spent here, living in the cabin, reminded him that he was a wounded combat vet, still dependent on his father's charity. It shamed him.

Using his cane, his father pushed slowly to his feet. "Everything okay?"

"No," Wyatt answered, a lump in his throat and a hot coal burning beneath his sternum. "It's a done deal. The Miller house is sold." And God, he was completely shredded inside.

He'd pinned so much on getting that house when it came up for sale, had refused offers of loans from friends and relatives who knew he wanted it. Ever since the house had become vacant he'd put away whatever money he could so he'd have the down payment ready when the estate decided to sell. All for nothing.

"Ah, damn, I'm sorry to hear that."

He nodded, pointed a thumb over his shoulder. "Piper's a minute or so behind me, so I'm sure we'll get the full story from her. I'd rather talk to her alone for a while, if you don't mind." It wasn't a request, even though he phrased it as one.

"Of course. Come on, boys," he told the dogs. Sarge waddled after him, but Grits stood there watching Wyatt, the end of his tail wagging.

"Go on," Wyatt said in a firm voice, pointing toward the house.

Grits lowered his head and his tail drooped, but he turned and followed Wyatt's dad. It made Wyatt feel like a dick but he just couldn't afford to let the dog into his heart.

Once in the solitude of his cabin Wyatt went directly to the cabinet to pull out the bottle of whiskey he hadn't touched in months, and a shot glass.

Two seconds later Piper's little red car parked in front of his porch. She walked up to his screen door wearing a worried expression and her workout clothes, her dark blond hair pulled back into a ponytail. "Hey," she said, her tone hesitant as she let herself inside.

"Hey."

"So, did you meet the owner?"

"Yep." And she had most definitely not been what he'd expected. At all. He'd had trouble keeping his eyes on her face during that whole exchange.

"And?"

"She's tall." Damn near as tall as him, not to mention strong and determined. And her long, toned body had been impossible to ignore, even for him and his black mood.

"That's it?" Piper asked in exasperation. "She's *tall*?"

He shrugged, keeping the rest of his observations to himself. Austen Sloan had smooth, creamy-brown skin, long, dark, spiral-curled hair, and eyes a surprising shade of light gray, almost silver. It annoyed the hell out of him that he'd even noticed how hot her body was. Not that Piper needed to know any of that.

"And, she won't sell. She says she's going to fix it up and stay there." It felt wrong to him on every level, a violation. That place should have been his.

"Well, at least we know she's not planning to rip it down."

"So she says. Once she realizes the amount of work and the costs involved, she might change her mind." His only hope now was that she might either change her mind partway through and sell it to him, or once she was done with it. It made his inner control freak cringe to think about what she might do to the place while she renovated it.

He'd had big plans, specific and *respectful* plans of how he'd renovate it, to preserve the character and charm, keep the heart of the home beating amongst all the updates. God, he hated the thought of anyone else touching it, let alone someone from outside the area who had no personal attachment to it.

"I heard she's a firefighter from out of state," Piper said.

He paused a second. "Really?" She had the build for it, and the thought of what she'd look like wearing her turnout gear was surprisingly hot.

She nodded. "Apparently she's been looking for a property in the area for a couple weeks now. Just shit luck that her agent called the estate lawyers at the right time." Piper plopped down in one of the kitchen chairs, rested her folded arms on the table and set her chin on top of them, looking as dejected as he felt. "I'm so sorry," she said, watching him with sad hazel-green eyes.

He knew she was, and that this wasn't her fault. If she could have gotten him the house somehow, she would have. "How the hell did this even happen?"

"I guess the other agent was in talks with the estate's lawyers over the past week or so. They never officially put in on the market so no one knew about it. Several of the beneficiaries had a meeting and convinced everyone to sell. Ms. Sloan's agent called them to inquire if they'd be interested in selling, saying she had a buyer who was willing to pay in cash."

"Cash? She paid for it outright?" It had to have set her back a pretty penny. The land itself was worth a lot because of the size and location, even without the house.

"Yes. They did the whole deal behind the scenes and I only found out about it yesterday."

This sucked so hard. "I would have paid them more." *But not in cash.* Banks liked cash, and no doubt so did the beneficiaries of the estate. "Why didn't they at least announce it was for sale and then wait to see if more offers came in?"

"Cash, and timing. I'm guessing the beneficiaries just wanted to liquidate the assets to cash them out. They've been sitting on the property for several years, I guess they got itchy and finally decided to pull the trigger when a cash sale offer fell in their lap." She paused, eyeing him with a hard look. "You weren't an asshole to her, were you?"

"I wasn't at my most charming," he admitted.

"Oh, God."

He rolled his eyes. "It wasn't that bad." He picked up the whiskey and poured a shot. The first of several he planned to knock back.

"Don't."

At the sharply spoken word he stopped and looked back at Piper. She was rigid in her seat, freckles standing out on her pale face, her expression pinched as she stared at him. "Getting drunk isn't going to solve anything."

Silently cursing himself, he sighed and set the bottle down. *Damn.* "I was just gonna have a shot or two, not drink the rest of the damn bottle," he said, turning away from it and folding his arms over his chest. It was no secret he'd drowned his problems with alcohol for the first couple months he'd moved home. Since then, he'd barely had anything to drink.

"Just…don't," she said, her voice rough, eyes filled with pain.

Hell, he hadn't even thought about what seeing him pouring shots would trigger for her, due to her piece of shit soon-to-be-ex-husband. He expelled a breath. "Sorry, I didn't think." Wyatt wished he'd punched the fucker's lying, manipulative face when he'd had the chance.

She flushed and glanced away, looking uncomfortable. "It's okay."

No, it wasn't, and he was a jerk for not remembering. He put the bottle and shot glass away. If he still felt the need for a drink later on, he could do it after she left.

An awkward silence settled between them in the still kitchen, but was thankfully filled by the sound of paws scrambling on the front porch. Grits jumped up to put his front paws on the screen door, tongue lolling, tail going like crazy as he stared at Wyatt.

"Hey, little man," Piper cried, getting out of her chair to open the door and scoop him up. She grinned when he immediately started licking her face. "Such a lover, even after all you've been through. How come none of my boyfriends were ever as good a kisser as you, huh?" She shot a teasing glance at Wyatt and he couldn't help but smirk. He'd been eighteen the last time he'd kissed her, and he was a hell of a lot better at it now than he'd been back then.

Not that he'd kissed or done anything else with a woman since being wounded. Women seemed to fall into two categories now, either pitying him or wanting to mother him. Both were major turnoffs.

He also didn't relish the thought of a woman seeing his amputation for the first time. No doubt a major turnoff for whoever his prospective bed partner was.

Piper sighed, buried her face in the dog's soft fur. "As crappy as things get in life, dogs always have a way of making it better, don't they? They're the masters of unconditional love."

They were. Wyatt didn't answer though, because he knew the question was rhetorical.

Shuffling footsteps crunching over gravel reached him a moment before his father came into view through the screen door. "Knock, knock."

Piper swung around with a big smile on her face. "Hey, Mr. C."

"Good to see you," his dad replied, his gaze cutting back and forth between them. "Tried to keep Grits with me, but he wasn't having it. He's pretty attached to you already," he told Wyatt, and there was a note of reproach there.

"I think he just wanted to see Piper," Wyatt muttered.

She shot him a glare. "He came here because *you're* here, because for whatever reason, he already loves your grumpy ass. I'm just a bonus." She held the dog out in front of her and gave him a big, open-mouth grin, her voice turning babyish. "Aren't I, Gritsy? A big, happy bonus." Grits answered with a series of licks as he wiggled in her hold, his tongue meeting nothing but air as he tried frantically to kiss Piper's face again.

His father's gaze shifted to him, unreadable. "Want me to take him back to the house?"

"Nah, it's fine." He could use a friend right now, and though Piper was great, he didn't want human company at the moment. Grits didn't expect him to talk, didn't ask questions or judge him. Even if he still hadn't decided if he would keep the little guy or not, the dog was sweet and easy to have around.

After raising one eyebrow at him in a *you're-not-fooling-anyone* gesture, his dad switched his attention to

Piper. "So, it's been a shit day around here so far. How's yours going?"

Piper set Grits down, her brightness fading. "Okay."

Wyatt exchanged a loaded look with him, because they both knew damn well her life at the moment was anything but *okay,* no matter how much she tried to act like it was.

His old man gave Piper a smile, and even lopsided due to the stroke it was still loaded with Colebrook charm. "I was just about to risk lighting the house on fire while I made myself a late breakfast. You care to join me? Give an old cripple a hand?"

Her gaze turned fond. It was no secret she loved his father to pieces, and vice versa. "You're far from a cripple, but I'd love that, thank you." She glanced at Wyatt. "You coming?"

"In a bit. Have to take care of my leg first." With all the chaos he hadn't had time to check and clean his stump and prosthesis since he got home this morning, and he needed to do it ASAP.

Being an amputee sucked, but being able to wear an artificial was a hell of a lot better than having to use crutches. Inspecting the stump and making sure the skin stayed clean and dry every day was essential to avoid infection that would prohibit him from using his prosthesis.

"Okay, but don't be too long," she said over her shoulder as she walked through his front door. "I want to hear more about Austen Sloan and what you plan to do about this."

What he planned to *do* about it? What could he do, when she'd already told him flat out she wouldn't be selling? He remained leaning against the counter, lost in his thoughts as his dad and Piper headed for the main house, arm-in-arm.

Was there a way to fix this? There had to be. Getting that house had been his dream for so long, now that it had been taken away from him he felt...empty. Lost, even.

No, worse than that. He felt like an utter failure at life.

Grits wandered over and sat in front of him, gazing up at him with those huge brown eyes. His gaze wasn't sharp and intelligent as Raider's had been, but rather soft and adoring. "What?" Wyatt asked him gruffly.

Unfazed by the tone, Grits swished his feathery white tail back and forth over the planks and tilted his head to one side, ears lifting.

Wyatt frowned at him. The adorably cute routine wasn't going to work on him. He didn't *want* to get attached to another dog. It was too soon, would feel too much like he was dishonoring Raider's memory. And for damn sure, he never wanted to feel the pain of losing his best friend ever again.

That's what Raider had been to him, and he didn't care if people didn't understand that. He'd been a dog person ever since he could remember, but once he'd joined the Marines and begun working with his own military working dog, that bond had been on a totally different level to anything he'd ever known.

Raider had slept beside him every night for over two years, had lain across Wyatt's body to stand guard while Wyatt slept when they were outside the wire, staying on alert for any sign of danger. He'd trusted that dog with his life, and with the lives of his fellow Marines, and Raider had depended on him to protect her. So when Raider had died that day because of Wyatt's mistake, it had shattered him. He'd never get over it, no matter how long he lived.

Against his will, his gaze strayed to the mantel, where the urn holding Raider's ashes sat in the center, next to a framed picture of them together and the collar Raider had been wearing that fateful day.

Guilt slashed at him as he looked back down at Grits, who sat watching him with a heartbreakingly hopeful expression. Staring into those warm brown eyes, Wyatt felt his resolve to stay detached soften a fraction.

The dog was too damn adorable. Poor little guy hadn't deserved the shit life he'd had up until he was rescued. What Wyatt wouldn't give for five minutes alone with the asshole that had kept him caged and made him skittish of people.

"I'm no good for you. Not right now, anyway," he told Grits, trying to hold firm.

Grits swished his tail even harder and Wyatt swore he could hear the dog's thoughts. *Please just give me a chance. I want to be your friend.*

He couldn't stand it.

Despite himself, Wyatt bent to scoop him up and held the dog against his chest. Grits's fur was so damn soft, his solid little body warm, and all he wanted was to be loved.

As if he knew he'd just put a major crack in Wyatt's defenses, Grits beat his tail in a joyful rhythm against Wyatt's belt buckle as his little pink tongue licked at the scruff on Wyatt's face that was well on its way to forming a short beard. Unconditional love, even after the way he'd been treated by humans for the first two years of his life.

Without a doubt, the best antidepressants in the world had four legs and a wagging tail. Even Wyatt and his demons didn't stand a fucking chance against that kind of medicine.

Holding the dog to him, he sighed, his voice rough as he spoke to the empty room. "So now what the hell am I gonna do with myself?"

Chapter FOUR

His personal monsters were out in full force tonight. Even worse than usual, and at this stage he'd assumed that wasn't possible.

Times like this made him wish he had the guts to kill himself and get it the hell over with. Anything to stop the memories and the cycle of self-destruction that had led him to this point.

Shutting his truck door behind him he headed through the garage into the house. The piece of shit house he was forced to rent because he'd lost pretty much everything.

In the kitchen he went straight for the bottle of Jack sitting on the counter. This time he didn't even bother pouring it into a glass, he just drank straight from the bottle, the burn igniting a mellow heat that spread out from the pit of his stomach.

After a few swallows he set it down and reached with a shaking hand for one of the prescriptions sitting next to the sink. The instructions warned not to consume alcohol with them, but fuck it. Mixing them hadn't killed him yet, and it was a risk he was more than willing to take. He craved the oblivion that only getting wasted could bring.

The nights were always the hardest, with mornings a close second, when everything hit him all over again. Now that he was alone there was nothing to quiet the static in his head. At this point he wasn't sure if the pain he felt was all in his head or not. The alcohol helped numb him for a little while, but tonight he planned to get good and shitfaced.

Glancing around the empty kitchen, the walls began to close in around him. Desperate to escape the loneliness and the memories that ate him alive, he shoved his way through the screen door and onto the back porch that looked out onto the tiny patch of grass he called a yard.

Above him the night sky stretched out in a blanket of black. Crickets sang in the distance as he watched the clouds pass over the face of the moon. A few months ago he'd lived in a four-thousand-square-foot home set on two acres of land. He'd had a wife, a beautiful wife—

No. He didn't want to think about that heartless bitch. She'd kicked him out of her life and moved on, telling him she was done with him and his addictions. She'd vowed to stand with him through sickness and health, but she hadn't meant it. Not really.

A wave of self-loathing and pity washed over him as he stood there surveying the state he now found himself in. His life was as fucked-up as he was, but nobody cared. Not his ex or his family. Not even his friends. Oh, they had sympathized at first, but now they all said this was his fault. That he'd brought all this on himself with the booze and drugs.

They didn't get it. Just because his wounds weren't visible didn't mean they weren't there.

It enraged him that people blamed him for the way his life had turned out. If he'd been like that damn Wyatt, with the marks of his personal demons right out there in the open for everyone to see, things would have been way different.

People in this town might pity Wyatt for what had happened to him, but at least they still respected him. But Wyatt was a Colebrook. A family that had been in the Valley forever and damn near revered by the people here. They had money, they had connections, things that made their lives so much easier than his.

He was sick to fucking death of hearing about them all, of having the wounded paragon that was Wyatt rubbed in his face every damn day.

The more he thought about it, the more bitter he became. Unlike Wyatt, no one respected him anymore. No one cared that his entire life was falling apart all around him. Here he was, stuck in this dump and scraping by from month to month, while Wyatt lived for free on his family's land.

And Piper always there to check on him.

Thinking of her made the knife of jealousy twist harder. She was beautiful, and always seemed to wind up coming out on top no matter what life threw at her, while he sank lower and lower.

He scowled up at the moon as the resentment grew. Why the hell did she still care about Wyatt so much? What power did he hold over her? Even after all this time she was always there for him, always calling or popping by with cookies and pie or whatever.

She went to Wyatt, while *he* suffered alone. It wasn't fair.

Rage built inside him, growing hotter with each passing minute. It was all Wyatt's fault. All of it. When he thought of that arrogant bastard he wanted to punch him in his scarred fucking face. He wanted to see the high-and-mighty Wyatt Colebrook hurt as much as he was hurting.

The tantalizing thought took root in his brain and wouldn't let go. It had been forming in there for a while but now it was irresistible. He could even the score. Make Wyatt suffer for everything he'd caused.

His steps were uneven as he staggered back into the house and down the peeling linoleum hallway to the room he slept in. A box and mattress sat on the stained carpet next to the footlocker he'd kept.

Kneeling in front of it, he undid the lock and opened the lid. With a shaking hand he reached in for the pistol sitting on top. He cleaned it every day and took it to the range at least four times a week, always made sure it was fully loaded and ready to go.

And he had other weapons too. Rifles and knives and various tools of the trade he kept for protection.

Now they could serve another purpose.

Sooner than later, he was going to die. Either by drinking himself to death, or from overdose. Maybe one day he'd eat a bullet, either by his hand or someone else's. Whatever form it took, his death was unavoidable and he knew it would happen soon.

But in the meantime, he didn't have to be the only one hurting.

A burst of excitement burned through his veins. He could make Wyatt suffer as much as he was. The bastard deserved it after what he'd done.

Gently he placed the pistol back on top of the articles packed into his footlocker, a plan slowly taking shape in his mind. Killing him was too easy. He wanted to show Wyatt what true pain felt like.

All he needed was to figure out Wyatt's greatest weakness. Then he'd know how to hurt Wyatt the most and make him pay for all the lives he'd ruined.

****

Austen lugged the last of the supplies she'd need for the day up to the counter of the hardware store and dug out her credit card as the man behind the counter rang everything up. The owner, a man in his early fifties she'd gotten to know a little bit over the past week.

"You sure got your hands full with that house."

"Don't I know it," she said with a wry smile. Every muscle in her body ached from all the work she'd put in already, toiling from morning until well past dark just to put a dent in it. In the end all her effort was going to be worth it though.

"Find a contractor yet?" he asked with a friendly smile.

"No, everyone I've called is booked up for months."

"Busy time of year for them."

Yeah, her timing kind of sucked. Of course there *was* one name that kept coming up over and over, although she had no interest in calling him.

Wyatt Colebrook.

Since their inauspicious introduction on her front porch last week she'd learned quite a bit more about his background from the locals who'd mentioned him to her. He'd been in the Marines and had lost his lower leg and an eye in an IED explosion in Afghanistan.

After coming home to Sugar Hollow he'd been helping his disabled father out on their family horse farm, and taking on contracting or renovation jobs here and there. At first it had surprised her that people had talked so openly about such personal details with an outsider, but she was getting used to it. Gotta love small towns.

According to the locals she'd talked with, Wyatt was one of the best builders around, though he didn't take on a lot of projects because of other things he had to juggle. His family was well-respected here in the Valley, had been here for generations, and he seemed to be well-liked.

That last part surprised her too, but it sounded like she'd gotten a bad impression of him and she supposed he had a right to be annoyed with her since she'd bought the house he'd wanted for so long. She wouldn't hold it against him.

Two of the guys working in the shop helped her cart everything out to her truck. So far she'd managed to do a chunk of the demo work on the main floor but the progress was painfully slow with just her doing the labor. Her hands were already blistered and her whole body hurt from wielding the sledgehammer for the better part of two days.

With her skills she could handle the bulk of the carpentry work on her own. She even knew the basics of electrical and some plumbing. But she needed a crew and licensed tradespeople to do the things she wasn't qualified to tackle. Trouble was, she had limited funds—she was using all her savings and John's life insurance settlement to do this—and everyone was booked.

Well, almost everyone.

Slamming the tailgate closed, her stomach rumbled and she stifled a yawn. The motel she was staying at was right on the freeway and not exactly soundproof. She knew far too much about the young couple in the room beside her, since they'd been up most of the night screaming at each other.

By three in the morning the epic fight had worried her enough that she'd almost called down to the front desk to have management intervene, but then things had quieted down. Immediately followed by the rhythmic thump of the headboard against the wall between their rooms.

Annoyed and embarrassed for them, Austen had rolled over and stuffed two pillows over her head to try and block out the sound, but it hadn't helped. This morning she hadn't been able to look either of them in the eye when she'd bumped into them as they left their room.

Stretching her stiff neck, she glanced down Main Street toward the *Garden of Eatin' Café*. This area of downtown was super cute with its pretty row of shops and restaurants, all the Victorian-style buildings restored to their original glory in a rainbow of colors, all decorated with gingerbread trim and covered porches. In the few days she'd been in town she'd already taken dozens of pictures of it to send to her friends back home.

No, that wasn't home, she reminded herself. *This* was home now.

And while she might be lonely, she liked it here and she knew she'd make friends soon enough. The people were friendly and the town was so quiet and peaceful, like something out of a painting. Once the house was completed she'd decide whether she wanted to go back to firefighting or maybe flip a few houses to make some money.

She waited for a truck to pass before crossing the street. From what she'd seen, the *Garden of Eatin'* did a steady stream of business all day long, seven days a week. She'd become a regular here already, stopping at least once a day for a snack or a coffee. Right now she was starving and needed something to fill her up so she could get some serious work done at the house.

The lineup was five people deep when she stepped inside, and the scents of freshly brewed coffee and homemade cinnamon cake made her mouth water. She perused the glass case at the front while she waited in line, then ordered a big slice of quiche along with a vanilla latte and a freshly made yogurt parfait to go.

Giving her order to the girl behind the counter, Austen thanked her with a smile and started to turn away.

"Austen."

She glanced to her right, spotted Piper, a real estate agent she'd met here at the café a few days ago. "Hey."

"Got enough to fuel you up for the day?" The end of her dark blond ponytail swished against the tops of her shoulders when she nodded at Austen's bag.

Austen smiled. "For a few hours, anyway." She was tall and had a solid build. It took a lot of fuel to keep her going.

"How's it going over there?" Piper asked, adding a sugar to her drink before eyeing Austen as she put the lid on.

"Slow. It's just me so far."

Piper took a sip of her coffee, raised her eyebrows. "Still no luck finding anyone?"

"No."

She frowned. "Did you talk to Wyatt about it yet?"

Piper had been one of the first to recommend him. "No, I only talked to him on the day I bought the house. He showed up to let me know he wasn't happy about it, and that he wanted to buy it back. I told him I wasn't interested."

Piper winced, her eyes full of sympathy. "Yeah, I heard."

Small towns. She had to remember that word traveled fast here. "So no, I haven't called him."

Piper motioned toward the front door and Austen followed her out onto the sidewalk into the cool May morning air. Warm golds and rosy pinks painted the eastern horizon where the sun was still hidden by the Blue Ridge Mountains, promising a gorgeous day.

"I think you should call him," Piper said. "I can imagine what you thought of him after the first impression you got, but he really is a good guy and he's awesome at what he does. His bark is way worse than his bite, trust me, and even though he doesn't take on a lot of contracting jobs, he might do this one."

"It sounds like you know him pretty well."

"We go way back," she replied with a dismissive wave of her hand. "He's gruff and intimidating at first, but once you get to know him a little you'll see right through all that. The man's got a big, marshmallowy heart underneath that crusty, alpha male exterior that he doesn't like anyone to know about, and he loves animals, especially dogs. So he's not all bad," she added with a grin.

Austen wasn't sure why Piper was telling her all this. "I think I'd feel too awkward having him work on the house. I can tell the place means a lot to him. The last thing I need is a bitter contractor to deal with." Asking him to do it would be like rubbing salt in his wound, and she wasn't that kind of person.

Piper nodded. "It does mean a lot to him. And that's a good thing, because if he agreed to take on the project, he'd make sure everything was done right. Believe me, he'd do a fantastic job. He's a perfectionist." Her phone rang and she pulled it out of her purse to check it.

Whatever showed on the screen made her face tighten and her shoulders tense. She flashed Austen a slight smile that didn't take the weariness from her eyes. "Sorry, I've gotta take this. Just think about what I said, okay? And call me if you have any more questions. Have a good one."

"You too."

"I've asked you not to call me," Piper said in a hushed tone as she walked away, clearly not wanting anyone else to overhear the conversation. "If you can't

41

respect me even that much, then I'll have to..." Her voice trailed off as she rounded the corner. But from what Austen had heard, yikes, it didn't sound good.

As she drove to the house, Austen weighed Piper's words about Wyatt and enjoyed the picturesque scenery she passed. The south side of town was filled with residential lots, most of the houses from the mid-to-late nineteenth century. People here took pride in their homes and their town, and it showed in the well-maintained lots, the pretty gardens bursting with colorful roses and clematis, the lawns neatly trimmed.

Here the tidy, quiet streets were lined with oaks, cherry trees and the sugar maples the town had been named after. She'd missed out on seeing the cherry blossoms this year, but the summer foliage was going to be gorgeous and she couldn't wait to see the explosion of color that would happen in the fall.

As she turned up her driveway and drove along the row of sugar maples lining either side, her heart filled with warmth at the sight of the grand old lady ahead of her. She was so in love with the property and wanted the house to reflect her vision once it was done. This was definitely a home to sink her heart into, and a place to put down roots in. To do that, she needed to hire some help.

Her first meeting with Wyatt hadn't been the friendliest, but this house wasn't fixing itself and she couldn't do it alone. If he really was as good as people said, then maybe it was worth at least calling him to see if he was interested. And, if he took the job, maybe getting to work on it would give him some sense of peace, once he saw that she intended to take good care of it.

Or not.

Parked in front of the sagging front porch, she sat there for a long moment, gazing up at the house. It really was a crime, the way this place had been let go. Its faded, peeling and frankly ugly mud-green paint cried out for help.

Well, the truth was they *both* needed help. A simple phone call wouldn't kill her.

Mind made up, she pulled out the business card he'd handed her and dialed Wyatt's number, trying to ignore the nervous flutter in the pit of her belly as she waited for him to answer. As far as conversations went, this was going to rate up there with the most awkward she'd ever had, but she was at the end of her rope and finding good help for this project took precedence over her pride.

Chapter FIVE

Wyatt didn't recognize the out-of-state number calling his cell phone. For a second he thought about ignoring it, then changed his mind. His youngest brother, Easton, was due in today. Maybe he was calling from a new cell phone or something. "Hello?"

"Mr. Colebrook?"

He paused in the act of pulling the fixings for a sandwich out of the fridge, that husky feminine voice somehow familiar. "Yes."

"This is Austen Sloan."

He set the mayo jar down before he dropped it. "Hi." For some reason, his heart skipped a beat at the sound of her voice. Why was she calling him? Had she changed her mind about the house?

"I just want to say up front that I still haven't changed my mind about selling, so don't get your hopes up."

Damn. At least she was candid about it. "Okay, fair enough." He was still hoping she'd change her mind in the end though.

"I need a contractor. You've been recommended to me repeatedly as one of the best around. I'm hoping me owning the house won't stop you from considering working with me on it."

Yeah, good call on putting the mayo jar down. "You want to hire me as your general contractor?" After the way things had gone between them, she had to be pretty desperate to reach out to him on this. She had balls to call him, he'd give her that.

"I might. I'd like to set up a meeting with you about it. If you're interested. I'd understand if it would be too uncomfortable for you, but I'm anxious to get going on this and I want it done right. From what I've heard, you're a perfectionist and you won't rip me off. Those are both pluses in my book."

He didn't know who she'd been talking to, but then a lot of people in the area knew him, or at least knew his family. "I'd be open to a meeting," he said cautiously. "When did you have in mind?"

She let out a soft laugh that did something to his insides. A stirring. "How about now?"

He thought about it for a moment, even looked down at Grits, who was of course at his feet, on the off chance that Wyatt dropped something in the middle of making his lunch. Could he stomach working on the house, knowing he didn't have a chance at owning it? And what if she wanted to do something he didn't agree with, like rip something down he thought should stay?

"I could meet you in a couple hours." He didn't want to seem too eager. He had a sandwich to eat, and then he needed to get cleaned up. "One o'clock?"

"Sure, I'll be here at the house. Does that work?"

"Yes. I'll see you then." He ended the call and slipped his phone back into his jeans pocket. "Have to be one hell of an offer, to get me to bite," he said to Grits, who wagged his tail and gazed up at him adoringly.

Now he was curious as to what her plans were, and whether she could afford him and his crew. Because that project wasn't going to be cheap, or fast. Wyatt got to work making his BLT, and "accidentally" dropped a few crumbles of bacon that Grits sucked up almost before they hit the floor.

After showering and taking care of his stump and prosthesis, he grabbed his laptop and a pad of paper before getting Grits's harness and leash out of the closet. "Wanna go in the truck?"

Ears perking up at the word *truck*, the dog raced over, ears flying, and stood wriggling in place while Wyatt slipped on the harness. He was a sweet little fella, but had absolutely no recall and a strong hunting instinct. Wyatt had already seen the dog had a tendency to chase things. A barn cat, a bird, and even a fly that had gotten trapped in the house the other day. Grits had chased it down for the better part of thirty minutes before giving up. No way Wyatt was letting him off leash in an unfenced area.

Outside he spotted Scott, one of the wounded vets he and his dad hired to help them around the property, heading out of the barn. "Possible job offer?" Scott asked him, indicating the notepad Wyatt held as he headed over.

"Maybe."

"In town?" He pushed his sandy brown hair out of his face.

"The old Miller place."

He stopped. "It sold?"

"Last week."

Scott winced. "Oh, man, I'm sorry."

Wyatt nodded. "Big job. Would keep us all busy for a few solid months at least."

"Well let's hope you get it then," he said with a grin and Wyatt was glad to see that spark of life in him. Lately Scott had seemed to be sliding back into depression, just one of the demons he wrestled with from a combination of PTSD and the brain injury he'd suffered in Afghanistan. His recent divorce hadn't helped matters any either.

Scott had missed work a few times over the past month, something that had cost him a few jobs before Wyatt had hired him. Since Wyatt had talked to him about it he'd been steady ever since and Wyatt and his dad were glad for the help around the farm.

In the Army Scott's MOS had been as an interior electrician, and he was damn good at electrical work, which was why Wyatt liked to hire him on building jobs. Steady work for a few months would give him and the other guys a purpose, a reason to get up each morning, and give them the satisfaction that came with putting in a solid day's work. He owed it to them to try and get this bid.

"I'll let you and the others know if anything comes of it," Wyatt said, and headed for his truck with Grits trotting beside him.

It took fifteen minutes to drive to the Miller place. As he turned up the driveway, he braced himself for the inevitable wave of heartache that hit him when the house came into view.

Grabbing his stuff, he lifted Grits down from the passenger seat and walked him up to the front porch. A little cute, furry backup was a welcome icebreaker right now.

Austen appeared in the front doorway as they reached the top step, and without the anger and fear tearing at him this time, her welcoming smile hit him right in the solar plexus.

Standing there before him, she seemed to glow from some inner light source. She had on a snug T-shirt that outlined the pert curve of her breasts, and faded jeans that hugged her long, strong-looking legs, her curly hair tied back into a ponytail.

"Hi there. Who's this?" That smile grew even wider as she crouched and reached a hand toward the dog, who stretched his head forward but didn't go toward her, tail down, just the end of it wagging. Unsure, but craving the affection she offered.

"Grits."

She looked up at him, those gorgeous silver eyes sending another jolt through him. He'd been so caught up in his own emotional reaction before, he hadn't realized just how pretty she was. "Grits?"

"I know. I didn't name him. He's a rescue."

Her expression melted as she looked back at the dog. "Hey, cutie. I won't hurt you. C'mere." She stayed absolutely still, hand held outward, palm up, her posture nonthreatening, and she didn't stare into Grits's eyes. Wyatt could tell a lot about a person by the way they acted around a dog, and so far, he liked what he was seeing in Austen.

He stood there watching her as she waited, and Grits took a cautious step forward, his tail rising slightly and gaining speed. The dog clearly wanted to meet her, but was still a little unsure. Her actions told Wyatt she was no stranger to dogs, and she obviously seemed to like them. More points in her favor.

"He's still a little unsure around strangers," Wyatt explained.

"It's okay." She stayed still, crooning softly to Grits for a few moments, the soothing sound of her voice stroking over Wyatt like a caress.

Grits stretched his neck out to sniff her upturned palm, then began licking it. Austen gently scratched the underside of his chin, knowing enough to not raise her hand to try and pet him on the top of the head, which would have frightened him. Three seconds after that, Grits practically climbed into her lap, his entire body wriggling, his tongue flicking like a lizard's at any part of her he could reach.

"Oh, he's so soft and sweet." Austen laughed and ruffled the white fur on Grits's chest. "So, does this mean we're friends now?"

"Think so." Wyatt couldn't help but smile. In his experience, dog lovers were good people. One more mark in Austen's favor, even if she had bought the house out from under him. Though to be fair, it wasn't like she'd known he'd wanted it.

She raised her eyes to his, gaze warm, and stood before holding out her right hand. He noticed there was a diamond ring on her finger, but her left hand was bare. "How about we start over? I'm Austen."

He accepted the handshake, unprepared for the shot of electricity that raced through him at the contact. "Hi. Nice to meet you again." He'd come here with the intent of being professional, nothing more, but she was being so nice he couldn't help wanting to be nice.

"You too." She withdrew her hand, glanced down at Grits. "Think he'd let me hold him now? I don't want him to step on any nails or anything sharp I've pulled out."

"I'm sure he would."

"C'mere, sweet baby," she crooned, bending to scoop him up. Grits all but melted into her hold, and Wyatt couldn't blame him. He felt like a jerk for the way he'd acted earlier, when she seemed like such a nice person. It wasn't like she'd connived to steal the house from him.

He cleared his throat, feeling stiff and awkward. Apologies had never been easy for him. "Listen, I'm sorry about how I was the other day."

She waved a hand. "I'm over it, so apology accepted."

He blinked, somewhat surprised she hadn't chastised him for his behavior or made him grovel a little more.

"Ready to see what I've got in mind?" she asked him.

"Sure." He followed her inside, a flood of bittersweet memories hitting him at the familiar smells of the old wood and the sights around him. It made him sad to see how bad the place had gotten.

"I'd like to start with the kitchen, then do the bathrooms. That way I can at least live here while the rest is being worked on."

He nodded, looking around. She'd taken the boards off all the windows, flooding the entry and kitchen with natural light. Judging from the pile of rubble already on the kitchen floor, she'd been busy.

Bits of mint green cabinets and speckled Formica countertop lay in heaps on the tarps she'd laid out. They'd been pretty much bombproof, so he knew what kind of muscle and time it would have taken to dismantle them. In addition to being a dog person, Austen Sloan also seemed to be a hard worker.

"I like the bones in here, so I'm not going to change anything structurally. I want to put in a small island along with the cabinets, and have a gasfitter install a line for the stove. I'm going to be doing the carpentry work myself," she told him, stopping in the center of the half-demolished kitchen.

Light filtering through the tall windows at the back of the kitchen brought out warm brown highlights in her dark hair. Her skin looked smooth and soft. So touchable. It had been forever since Wyatt had touched a woman that way, and this one was off limits.

"Okay," he answered, surprised and impressed that she could handle that herself. "You a carpenter?"

"Sort of. I did it on the side for years, but I was a firefighter for the past nine years."

"I heard."

She appeared surprised for a second, then she smiled. "Gotta love small towns. I'm still getting used to how things operate here. Way different than back in Philly."

"Yeah." Philly, huh? "You planning to work as a firefighter here?"

"Not sure yet. I want to get my feet under me for a while."

He wanted to know why she'd come here in the first place but held off on asking. That was too personal and he was here to do a job, not get to know her, even if his social graces weren't rusty. Which they definitely were. "Want to show me what else you have in mind?"

"Sure." Carrying Grits, she took him through the entire house, giving Wyatt a general idea of her vision.

The tight band that had been squeezing his ribcage eased a little more with each room they toured, because it was obvious she cared a great deal about restoring the house and doing a good job of it. He asked dozens of questions about the materials she had in mind, what kind of finishing.

Halfway through the upstairs tour, he got a text. Reading it, he frowned, and for a moment wondered if maybe Easton was playing some kind of twisted joke on him.

I'm watching you. How does it feel to be hunted?

What the hell? Someone either had the wrong number or was playing a prank on him, and he didn't have time for either. He was about to ignore it and put the phone back into his pocket when another message came in.

I'm going to make you pay for all the lives you've ruined.

At that he went dead still. Definitely not Easton. And the wording sent a chill down his spine.

His first impulse was to ignore it, but he couldn't. It hit too close to home, made him wonder if someone was referring to his past. And he didn't have the first clue who would send him anything like that. *Who the hell is this?* he fired back.

A reply came in a few seconds later. *By the time you find out, it will be too late.*

Fuck this.

He blocked the number and put the phone away, oddly shaken by the blatant threat and telling himself he'd look into this more later. When he looked back up, Austen was watching him with those startling silver eyes.

"Everything okay?" she asked.

"Yeah, I'll get back to them later." The words were already burned into his brain. If he found out who it was, he'd make them sorry they'd ever decided to mess with him. "Keep going."

"Like I was saying, I'd like to have the master bathroom attached, and add another full bath down the hall, which will mean losing one of the guest rooms."

Wyatt followed her down the narrow hall they'd have to widen, making note of the things she listed. It was hard not to stare at the shapely curve of her ass and her long legs, but he made sure she couldn't see him doing it and it helped distract him from those texts, at least for the moment. From what he could tell she didn't plan to change the overall structure except to take down a few partition walls to open up a couple of the rooms.

"Everything's going to need to be gutted and taken right down to the studs," she said as they stepped out of the upstairs bathroom. "The electrical and plumbing are ancient, and even though I've had everything inspected, we'll need to check the structure for stability as we go."

Nodding, he jotted down more notes on his pad. "What's your budget like?" Because all this was going to be expensive, and budgets tended to balloon with something this big.

At that she tensed, and the inner glow he'd noticed in her seemed to dim a bit. "It's tight. I can afford the materials, but I might not be able to cover all the labor. Whatever I can't pay to have done, I'll have to finish myself. That's another reason I called you. I heard you have a good reputation in terms of being fair, and not ripping people off. I'm hoping me owning the house won't affect your quote."

He shook his head. "I wouldn't do that. I'm honest."

Her lips curved into a slight smile. "That's pretty rare, in my experience." She scratched Grits's chest with her free hand. "So, what do you think? I know it's a lot to take on. Will you consider it and give me a quote?"

He wasn't going to walk away now that he understood what she wanted to do with the place. He could still put his stamp on the house, metaphorically rebuild some of what he'd destroyed. It was better than nothing and would have to be enough. "I'll take this home and work on it today. As soon as I have an estimate I'll call you, and I'll be sure to work with your budget as much as I can."

"Great." Relief flooded her face.

"And you should also know, I hire veterans pretty much exclusively."

"Sure, that's fine. I heard you were in the Marine Corps."

"Thirteen years." He'd intended to be a lifer like his dad…right up until the day he'd been wounded.

Wyatt waited, expecting her to ask about his scars now, but she didn't. That surprised him, but then maybe someone in town had already told her what had happened to him.

"My guys are all either wounded or disabled to some degree," he added. Some people weren't comfortable with that, and that was their prerogative, but if she was one of them, he wouldn't take the job.

"As long as you can vouch for them and their work, that's fine by me." No hesitation, no hint of concern about having potentially traumatized military-trained men showing in her expression, the way a lot of other people did. She was making it damn hard for him not to want this job.

He had no further questions and had hours of work ahead of him to put together the quote. "Great. So, can I have my dog back now?" Well, his dog for now, anyway.

Chuckling, she hugged Grits to her, kissed the top of his soft little head. "I dunno, he's so adorable, I just might steal him from you."

Maybe once this job was done, if he thought it would be a good fit, Wyatt might consider letting Austen adopt Grits. Right now, the dog was his to look after. Wyatt took him when she handed him over, got some sloppy kisses on the chin by way of greeting. "He's a licker." Nothing he'd said or done so far had broken the dog of the habit.

"Yes, I see that," she said on a laugh, and followed him out to the front porch. "Thanks for coming out on such short notice. I'm sure it wasn't easy for you, but I appreciate you taking the time to hear me out and consider the job."

Her words seemed genuine, and he appreciated the way she'd acknowledged his predicament without making a big deal of it. "You're welcome. I'll be in touch soon."

"Okay. Bye, Grits," she called out as Wyatt reached the gravel of the driveway.

Once in the cab of his truck, his cell buzzed with another text. Steeling himself, he pulled it out and read the message.

You can't get rid of me by blocking a number. You can't escape. I'm coming for you.

A twinge of unease hit him. Whoever this asshole was, he was persistent. Wyatt would call his sister, Charlie, to see if she or any of her tech buddies could find out who the caller was.

Though he doubted anyone would be dumb enough to threaten him and not take precautions to cover their tracks. As a former Marine, with one brother the team leader of one of the FBI's Hostage Rescue Team sniper units, and another on the DEA FAST team, a potential stalker would be nuts to target him.

Then again, whoever was behind this likely wasn't playing with a full deck to begin with. Keeping that thought firmly in mind, he put his phone away and started his truck.

As he drove away from the house with Grits perched beside him on the front passenger seat, he glanced up into the rearview mirror. Austen stood on the porch, watching him. If he was honest, she looked good there. The place suited her. And he was glad she cared about the property so much.

He pushed out a long breath and considered his next move. The house and the Miller family meant enough for him to take on this project. That way he could ensure he did everything possible to restore the house and preserve at least some part of the family's memory.

Of course, the prospect of getting to see its intriguing, sexy owner on a daily basis wasn't too much of a hardship, either.

Grinning to himself, he reached over and rubbed the top of Grits's head. "Things might be looking up after all, buddy." Those creepy-ass texts aside, his second meeting with Austen had gone way better than the first.

He was already looking forward to seeing her again next time.

Chapter SIX

Austen hefted another armful of debris into the Dumpster next to the front porch and paused to wipe the back of her wrist across her sweaty face. Her T-shirt was stuck to her back and chest, beads of sweat trickling down her forehead and it wasn't even noon yet.

The humidity here was surprisingly bad for May. She had no AC in the house yet, since they were still in the process of stripping out all the old electrical system, so the only ventilation was provided by the open windows and doors.

In short, this was gonna be a hell of a long day for all of them. But hey, at least she had help. Wyatt had called with a quote four days ago. She'd looked the numbers over, decided they were fair, and accepted. He and his crew had started the next day.

She trudged back up the steps on the front porch, past one of the guys who was prepping the exterior for paint, scraping off the old layers and giving everything a good sanding. Inside, two guys from Wyatt's crew were helping her gut what was left of the kitchen.

Scott and Eddie were both combat-wounded vets, but their injuries weren't visible like Wyatt's and the others' were. Everyone had been polite and respectful so far but the intent way Eddie watched her sometimes gave her the creeps.

Aside from that he seemed to be a hard worker and Wyatt had vouched for each guy on the crew he'd brought with him, so that made her feel better. She just made sure she was never alone in a room with Eddie, and gave him a wide berth whenever she could.

Scott and Eddie both stopped their demo of one of the kitchen walls when she came in, their arms and faces glistening with sweat and coated with powdery drywall dust. "Man, it's so humid today," Scott groaned, mopping at his face with the hem of his shirt.

"I know," she said, dreading what the humidity would be like in July and August. "Wyatt went to get us another generator so we could hook up a few room fans. He should be back soon."

"Not soon enough," another guy said as he hit the bottom of the main staircase. "It's gotta be over a hundred degrees up in that attic."

Austen winced in sympathy. At this rate, her crew would be completely melted and useless by lunchtime. "I'm gonna make a drink run to the café," she announced. The guys brought their own drinks and she had cases of water and Gatorade for everybody on site but the ice in the cooler was already melted and she wanted to get them something cold. "What do you guys want?"

She took everyone's order—seven in all—and jumped in her truck, feeling only slightly guilty as the AC blasted out of the vents all over her hot face and neck. At the *Garden of Eatin'* she placed the orders and picked up fruit salad and other refreshing snacks for the guys. Piper was just pulling into a parking spot out front when Austen came out.

"Feeding a crowd?" Piper asked her, smoothing her hands over the charcoal-gray pencil skirt that hugged her hips and thighs. Her makeup was light and tasteful but there were shadows beneath her eyes that even makeup couldn't conceal. Was everything okay?

"I'm worried the guys at the house are gonna melt on me. Melted crews aren't productive."

Piper's hazel eyes brightened, making the shadows less noticeable. "Oh, you found someone?"

"Wyatt. It's his crew."

A bright smile lit up her face. "That's great news. You won't regret it."

"Drop on by whenever you like. And when it's all done, I'd love to have you over to see the finished product."

"I'd love that, thanks."

Austen drove back to the house, making the most of the remaining minutes of air conditioning. When she turned down the driveway her heart gave a quick little leap at the sight of Wyatt climbing out of his truck, his broad shoulders outlined by the snug fit of his light gray T-shirt, and a pair of well-worn jeans hugging his sexy butt.

The man certainly revved her dormant libido. It took her off guard since she hadn't been attracted to anyone since John died, and because Wyatt didn't exactly seem overly fond of her. He was quiet and serious, had a gruff way about him, was all business around her.

She parked beside him just as he hefted the generator out of the bed of his truck, giving her an eyeful of the way the muscles in his arms and chest bulged. She'd worked around fit men most of her life, but something about Wyatt made her belly flutter in the most delicious way. All this time she'd thought that part of her had died along with John, but maybe not.

Climbing out with the trays of food and drinks, she smiled when she saw Grits sitting in the driver's seat of Wyatt's truck, watching her. "Brought your furry copilot with you, huh?" she said to Wyatt.

"Cavaliers are really prone to separation anxiety, and he's already had a rough start so I figure it's best that I just bring him with me."

"Uh huh," she said in a dry voice. After what Piper had told her, she wasn't buying the detached, analytical act. Not when it came to Grits, anyhow. "And it's got nothing to do with him being an adorable little sweetheart who thinks the earth revolves around you."

The hint of a grin twitched at the corners of his mouth, the closest thing he ever gave to a smile. That intrigued her too, made her wonder what it would take to make him laugh. She had no doubt that seeing a real smile from him would take her breath away. "Nope."

"Course not," she murmured. "I just did a drink run and I wasn't sure what you'd want so I picked you up a sweet tea at the café. I noticed you drinking one the other day."

"I appreciate it, thanks." He nodded toward the house, the muscles in his arms bulging as he held the generator with apparent ease. It had been forever since a man had held her, and the thought of those strong arms wrapped around her filled her with a deep longing that surprised her. "Just gonna get this set up so we can get the fans going."

"Perfect." She let him go first, stood there a moment to admire the flex of the muscles in his back and ass as he hauled the piece of equipment into the house. Didn't it figure that her libido would suddenly come back to life for a man who wanted nothing to do with her outside of a paycheck?

Watching him, it was hard to tell he'd lost his foot and lower leg. He never hinted that it was bothering him, never let it stop him or even slow him down, at least as far as she could tell. He oversaw everything in a quiet, methodical way, yet the biggest thing she noticed about how he worked was his calmness.

Maybe it came from his time in the Marines or from being in combat, she wasn't sure, but he had an innate confidence that drew people to him. Without a doubt he was a natural leader. He didn't expect anything of his guys that he wouldn't do himself, and it was obvious that they all looked up to him.

She'd worked with people like him before as a firefighter, but in her experience, leaders like that were rare. Seemed like Piper was right. Hiring Wyatt and his crew was the best thing she could have done for herself since moving to Sugar Hollow.

After dropping off drinks and food to all the guys, she headed outside to carry in one of the fans while Wyatt took the other and Grits pranced at his feet. "You okay carrying that?" Wyatt asked her. "It's heavy."

"I'm good," was all she said, shouldering the industrial-sized fan and hauling it inside. If she hadn't been so used to questions like that from guys, it might have annoyed her. Even men she'd worked with at the fire hall had questioned her ability to handle the physical demands of the job at first, but she'd quickly proved them wrong.

Wyatt's phone rang and she noticed the tight look on his face when he spoke to whoever it was. He even stepped out onto the porch to talk to the person, and his expression made it clear he didn't like what he was hearing.

"Everything okay?" she asked when he came back inside a minute later.

He nodded and got to work setting up the other fan without looking at her. "Just some news I was waiting on."

Not happy news, that much was obvious.

He didn't elaborate and she didn't press, although she wanted to. Wyatt was tough to read. He'd softened toward her somewhat since starting the job, at least compared to the first time they'd met, and she didn't want to lose any of the ground she'd gained with him by sticking her nose where it didn't belong.

"How are the guys doing? You feeling good about their work so far?" he asked as he connected some extension cords.

She reached down to pat Grits, who had run over to insert himself between her open knees as she set up one of the fans. "So far, so good," she answered, declining to mention that Eddie made her uncomfortable sometimes. If it got too bad she'd tell him. "Everything lining up okay with the tradespeople?"

"Mostly. Still a few gaps here and there. Did you go over that list I gave you?"

The list containing options for various materials he'd given her yesterday. Mostly she was concerned with cost and wanted to opt for the least expensive materials, but in some cases that could turn around and bite her in the ass later. Cheaper wasn't always better in the long run. "Almost done. Just a couple more things for me to look into."

"I'd like to talk about them as soon as possible, so I can order everything and have it here in plenty of time."

She nodded. "This afternoon?"

He shook his head. "I've gotta take my dad to an appointment."

"Oh. Maybe over dinner?"

At that he stiffened and his face went rigid, almost as if she'd hit a sore spot. "I don't really like eating out."

"Oh," she said again. *Why not?* "I'd offer to cook but my kitchen's not all that functional right now." As she said it, Eddie and Scott started back up with their sledgehammers.

One side of Wyatt's mouth pulled up in a sexy grin and his eyes met hers, sending a shock of awareness through her. "Yeah, I guess not. I could... You could come over to my place if you want. I'm not a good cook, but I can pick us up something."

"No need, I'll grab us dinner and bring it over."

Wyatt stood, shaking his head. "No, I'll do it. What do you like?"

She shrugged. "I'm easy. Whatever you like is fine by me. What time?" She pushed a sweaty strand of hair out of her face, could just imagine how she must look— the texture of her hair gave it a mind of its own and right now it had to be all frizzy, like she'd stuck her finger in a light socket.

"Seven."

"Okay. Where do you live?"

"I'll text you the address." He flipped the switch on the fan she'd just put up. Immediately a rush of cool air washed over her.

She closed her eyes and let out a heartfelt sigh of appreciation. "God, that feels good." When she opened her eyes her pulse tripped when she saw him watching her, an expression of pure masculine hunger on his face that disappeared so fast she wasn't sure if she'd imagined it.

He cleared his throat, looked away. "I'll go set this one up in the attic for Barry," he said, grabbing the other fan. "Come on, Grits."

Kneeling there on the floor she watched him go, and told herself it was the cool rush of the fan that made her break out in goose bumps and pebbled her nipples against the cups of her bra, not that look she'd just seen from the hard, sexy man walking away from her.

****

At six she called it a day and packed up her tools. Her back ached and she no doubt stank of sweat but it had been a good day.

The crew had left thirty minutes ago and between all of them they'd managed to do most of the demo on the main floor in just three days. The electrician Wyatt had hired was due in tomorrow to get things started, and the plumber a few days from now, along with the HVAC people.

Back at her motel room she stepped under the spray of a lukewarm shower that felt like heaven against her sweaty skin and scrubbed herself clean. Shaved, shampooed and moisturized, she put on a sleeveless, pale yellow sundress and open-toed sandals that showed off her pedicured toes.

It's not a date, she told herself as she applied light eye makeup in the bathroom mirror. Still, she wanted to look her best. And if tingles raced through her belly every time she thought about that hungry look on Wyatt's face, she couldn't help it. The man was sexy despite his gruff exterior and she was insanely curious about him.

To the west, the setting sun painted the sky in bold strokes of ruby and pink as she drove down the country road to the address Wyatt had texted her. The countryside out here was nothing short of spectacular, all rolling green fields nestled against the mountains.

Turning right at the driveway marked by the mailbox reading *The Colebrooks*, she caught her breath when the main house came into view. The rosy light from the sunset made the yellow two-story farmhouse glow. Its grounds were immaculate, the garden beds out front tidy and the grass cut.

Beyond the house, pastures bordered either side of the property, and a paddock sat out front of a wide red barn. To the right of it sat the cabin Wyatt lived in, a miniature version of the main house, complete with a wraparound porch enclosed by a white-painted railing.

Snagging the bottle of white wine from the passenger seat, she smoothed down the skirt of her dress and tried to ignore the nervous flutter in the pit of her stomach. The moment she stepped onto the front porch she heard Grits barking, then his little face appeared on the other side of the screen door. His ears lowered in recognition, his body swaying with the force of his wagging tail.

"Hey, little man. Is your human home?"

"Right here." Wyatt appeared in the opening, dressed in a dark-button down shirt and a pair of dark jeans. A surge of arousal hit her as she took in the sight of him, those big shoulders practically filling the doorframe. "Come on in."

She swept past him, getting a whiff of his clean, masculine scent that made her pulse beat faster. The entryway led directly into a kitchen that was small but clean, and being alone with him here felt intimate.

She held out the bottle, put on a smile. "I'm not sure if you drink it, but I brought us some wine."

"Oh. Thanks." He took it from her and went to a cabinet next to the fridge. "You want some?"

"Love a glass, thanks." She glanced around the space, taking in the layout. "It's so cozy and bright in here." Off the kitchen sat a living room with a rock fireplace, and beyond that, a porch that overlooked the fields beyond.

"Best part is the view off the back porch. We can sit out there after we eat."

"Sounds good. What are we having?"

His lips twitched again. "Italian takeout."

"Yum. My favorite." She accepted the wineglass with a murmur of thanks. "Can I help with anything?" She got the feeling he didn't often invite people over for dinner.

"No, just make yourself at home while I get everything set out."

Austen sipped at the crisp, cold wine as she wandered through into the living room. She loved the feel of the cabin, masculine without being unwelcoming, and snug. Her gaze caught on some pictures set on the mantel above the fireplace. An urn sat in the center of it, a dog collar wrapped around it.

Stepping closer, her heart lurched when she saw the framed photo of Wyatt before he'd been wounded. He was dressed in his combat utilities, on one knee beside a shepherd-breed military dog. God, just look at him. A true all-American hero. He was wearing sunglasses, a wide, proud smile stretching across his smooth, clean-shaven face.

Seeing him like that, prior to the hell he must have endured after being wounded, sent a sharp pain through her chest. Realizing what the urn held put an unexpected lump in her throat.

His quiet footfalls sounded behind her. She glanced over her shoulder to see him paused in the doorway, his expression unreadable. "Was this Raider?" she asked of the picture, using the name etched into the urn.

Wyatt nodded. "Lost her in Afghanistan. The day this happened." He gestured to the scarred side of his face.

"I'm sorry. What kind of dog was she, a shepherd?"

"No. Belgian Malinois."

She didn't know much about the breed, except that they were used a lot by military and law enforcement. "I'm sorry," she repeated softly, wishing she knew what else to say. "That must have been hard." As soon as she said it she mentally cringed. Seriously? That sounded so stupid, even though it had been sincere.

A muscle flexed in his jaw, then he nodded. "Yeah." He straightened, his posture and expression making it clear the topic was closed. "You hungry?"

Wishing she could somehow undo the last two minutes, she nodded and followed him into the kitchen, determined to try and salvage the rest of the evening.

Chapter SEVEN

Throughout dinner Wyatt tried not to stare at Austen but he couldn't help being distracted every time her lush lips closed around a forkful of food. Damn she was sexy, even more so because she seemed unaware of it.

Seeing her on his front porch earlier in that pretty yellow dress that showed off her toned arms and legs had kindled the hunger inside him. She'd left her hair down, all those springy dark curls bouncing around her shoulders and making him wonder if they'd wrap around his fingers if he ran his hand through them. In the overhead light above the kitchen table her creamy brown skin seemed to glow, her dark lashes making the silver-gray color of her eyes even more vivid.

She twirled pasta around her fork and slid it between her lips, her eyes meeting his. They crinkled slightly at the corners as she smiled and he was glad there was no lingering awkwardness after the abrupt end to their brief conversation about Raider. He didn't like talking to people about his military working dog, or that day, because experience had shown that civilians didn't understand, and they said stupid things in an attempt to make him feel better, when in reality it just pissed him off.

"This is really good, thanks," Austen murmured when she'd swallowed the mouthful. Her tongue darted out to lick some sauce from her lower lip and all he could think about was reaching across the table to slide his fingers into her hair and do the licking for her.

That was never going to happen, since she was technically his boss and that would spell disaster. Besides, he wasn't relationship material. He'd closed himself off from everyone but family, and didn't know if he'd ever be ready to open himself up again.

"You're welcome. It's a lot better than what I'm capable of in this kitchen, that's for sure." He could boil pasta and heat up jarred sauce, but he'd wanted to feed her better food than that.

She raised her wineglass to her mouth with her right hand and again his gaze caught on the ring on her third finger. It looked like an engagement ring but he wasn't sure what it signified that she didn't wear it on her left hand.

"What brought you to Sugar Hollow, anyway?" he asked.

She shrugged, drawing his attention to the way the top of her dress pulled taut over her breasts. "I was looking for some place small and quaint to settle down in." Twirling up more pasta, she added, "I'm here to start over."

Running from a bad relationship? The thought ignited a spark of anger in his gut. If some asshole had hurt her or scared her so much that she'd left Philadelphia and come here to start over, then—

"I lost my fiancé a couple years ago. I'd planned to stay in Philly, but as the months went by I felt the need to go someplace new, away from everything."

Oh. Hell. "I'm sorry."

She nodded, forced a smile. "Thanks." She glanced at the ring on her finger, frowned a little as her thumb toyed with it. "He was a firefighter too, but we were on different crews. I got a call on my first night off after finishing a rotation, saying that his crew had been responding to a fire when part of the ceiling had collapsed on them." She drew a breath, let it out slowly. "He held on for a couple of days, then…"

Unable to keep from touching her, he reached across the table to grip her hand, gave it a squeeze. "I'm sorry. You don't have to talk about it."

"No, it's okay." She met his eyes, her fingers curling around his in a warm grip. "Losing him was the hardest thing I've ever gone through, but thankfully it doesn't hurt as much as it used to. I've mostly learned to live with his memory, instead of letting it tear me apart. And it's easier for me to talk to you about it because you didn't know him."

Yeah, and he also knew what loss felt like. First his mom, then his Marine brothers and Raider. It sucked each and every time, plain and simple.

Nodding, he squeezed her hand gently before releasing it, a part of him wishing he had a reason to hold on instead. "It fades, but it never goes away."

She blew out a breath. "Exactly." She took another sip of wine. "Anyway, that's how I ended up here. John and I used to flip houses on the side. Smaller projects, nothing like the one you and I are working on now. We'd always dreamed of renovating a Victorian. So when I saw the Miller place and found out the owners were willing to sell, I used the money from John's life insurance policy and most of our savings to buy it." She gave him a rueful smile. "Yep, I'm all in, for better or worse. But I never meant to buy it out from under you."

He'd never expected this, hadn't even considered she'd been through something like that. God, now he felt like a total jerkwad for the way he'd acted the first time he'd met her. "Honestly? If anyone besides me was going to end up with it, I'm glad it's you. You deserve it and it suits you. We're gonna restore it exactly the way you want." He wouldn't settle for anything less, out of professional pride, but especially now that he knew her story.

The corners of her mouth lifted in the hint of a smile. "That's really big of you, Wyatt. I appreciate that."

He shrugged, uncomfortable with the praise, and decided this was the perfect opportunity to change the subject. "You bring that list with you?"

"Right here," she answered, pulling the papers out of her purse.

They were well into the second page when headlights flashed across the front window and the sound of a speeding vehicle broke the quiet. Frowning, Wyatt stood just as the driver plunged to a rocking stop out front.

As the driver flew out of the vehicle, Wyatt caught a glimpse of the man's face in the glare of the headlights and a hard ball of dread clenched in the pit of his stomach.

"Stay here," he told Austen, and immediately moved to intercept his unwelcome guest.

She turned in her seat but did as he said as he stalked to the front door. Greg was already on his way up the steps, but stopped when Wyatt came through the door. "What the hell are you doing here?" Wyatt demanded.

Greg had paused on the lower step but now he advanced, not stopping until he was face-to-face with Wyatt, only a few feet separating them. The former sheriff's body was as tight as his expression, blue eyes narrowed in a menacing glare as he thrust an accusatory finger at Wyatt. "You stay the hell away from my wife."

Huh? "She's not your wife anymore," he said quietly, barring Greg's way to the door. This confrontation was a long time coming and Wyatt wasn't about to back down from this pathetic asshole, even if he was sorry Austen had to witness it.

Greg paled at the verbal punch, then a flush of anger suffused his cheeks. Guy looked like shit, all rumpled and bleary-eyed, and Wyatt could smell the booze on him. "Yes, she is, and if you would stay the fuck out of it, she'd come back to me."

Aware that Austen was inside and could hear every word, Wyatt held back what he really wanted to say. "You're drunk, Greg, and probably high. There's nothing going on between Piper and me. You shouldn't be driving, but just go home."

"Fuck you," Greg spat, his face contorting with rage. "Fuck you and your high-and-mighty, holier-than-thou Colebrook attitude. It's your fault this happened. She never would have left me if it wasn't for you." His lips twisted into a sneer that only made him uglier. "Every damn time something went wrong, I had to hear about how I didn't measure up, how I would never compare to you. I've spent my entire life living in your shadow, and I'll be damned if I'll lose my wife over you."

Wyatt barely resisted the urge to scrub a hand over his face. Whatever the drugs and alcohol had done to Greg were the least of his worries. The dude had serious mental issues that went way beyond addiction. Piper hadn't left him because of Wyatt, she'd left him because he treated her like shit and couldn't stay clean. "I don't know what the hell you're talking about, but you've got five seconds before I make you get back in your car and leave. Go home and sleep it off."

Greg's fuse snapped. The man's dark blue eyes burned with a sudden fury. His face contorted and he reared one arm back. Wyatt shot out a hand to block the punch, catching Greg's fist and pushing him sideways.

Greg lost his balance, stumbled and caught himself against the railing. "Fuck you!" he snarled, and charged.

Wyatt braced himself, caught Greg's wrist when he got close enough, and whipped his arm up and behind his back. Grits barked hysterically behind him at the screen door. If it had been Raider, she would have torn through the screen door to get to him, and then torn into Greg.

Greg snarled and tried to whirl but Wyatt had already used the man's momentum against him, spinning him around and grabbing his other arm, pinning both behind him.

Enraged, Greg thrashed in his hold. "Let me go, you asshole! Let me go and fight me like a man, goddamn it!"

Wyatt was aware of Austen pushing her way through the screen door. "No," he told her sharply, struggling to hold Greg in place. He didn't want her getting hurt because of this drunken prick.

He was saved from asking her to call the cops by running footsteps coming across the gravel driveway. His brother Easton materialized out of the darkness, his expression livid as he ran for Greg.

"What the hell's going on?" Easton demanded, grabbing Greg's shoulders and muscling him to the porch floor with Wyatt.

"He's drunk and came here looking to pick a fight," Wyatt said, leaning over to hold onto Greg's wrists in a crushing grip. Not for the first time, he felt awful that Piper had to deal with this sorry son of a bitch on an almost daily basis until the divorce went through.

Greg tried to rear his head back, still struggling against their holds. Easton slammed him harder against the porch, leaned down to snarl at him. "*Enough.*"

Breathing hard, Greg stilled, his face dark red, pale green eyes shooting sparks.

"You stay down and cool off," Easton snapped, one knee digging into the middle of Greg's spine, "or we're calling the cops."

After a few seconds the man relented and went limp beneath them. Wyatt allowed Easton to take Greg's wrists and slowly eased away. His pulse raced, all his muscles locked and ready for more as he stood. Easton followed suit, watching Greg carefully as the man got to his hands and knees, then climbed to his feet.

Giving Wyatt a death glare, he jerked on the hem of his button down, jaw tight, eyes burning with the promise of retribution. "This isn't over," he rasped out, and started for the stairs. Easton automatically reached out a hand to stop him but Greg knocked it away and rushed for his car.

Easton cursed and started after him but Wyatt grabbed Easton's arm as the engine started up. The last thing they needed was for Greg to make this uglier and pull a weapon. "Let him go. I'll call the cops. He's wasted and I don't want him going after Piper."

"The cops won't get him in time," Easton said, his voice full of frustration. "I'll follow him, make sure he leaves her alone."

Wyatt handed him the keys, called out to him as Easton ran for Wyatt's truck. "Good to see you, little brother."

"Yeah, you too," Easton called back, raising a hand in acknowledgment as he jumped into the truck and chased after Greg.

Watching as Easton left, Wyatt called the cops and told them what was going on. The truck's taillights disappeared out of sight up the road as he ended the call and took a deep breath, letting it out slowly.

The screen door creaked open and he turned to see Austen there, holding Grits to her chest. She set the dog down and came up beside Wyatt, reaching out to wrap her fingers around his hand.

"You all right?" she asked softly. In the quiet he could hear the crickets singing in the grass. He took a deep breath and relaxed his muscles, let the peacefulness wash over him.

It was strange to be able to look her in the eye without bending his neck. Strange, but nice. She smelled damn good, a light mix of vanilla and something exotic that made him want to bury his face against her throat and breathe her in. "Yeah. Sorry you had to see that."

"Who was that?"

"Piper's ex."

"Piper?" she echoed in a shocked voice.

He nodded, still having a hard time believing Piper had ever seen anything good in that piece of shit. "The other guy was my youngest brother, Easton. He's going to make sure Greg stays away from her, and the cops will handle everything else."

"He's...unstable."

"Yeah, and out of his damn mind. I keep telling her to get a restraining order against him but she's been trying to avoid things getting uglier by keeping everything quiet." He met her gaze. "You've only been here a couple weeks, but surely you can see how fast word spreads around here."

She nodded.

"Well, gossip spreads even faster. The former sheriff and decorated Army vet coming here to start a drunken fight over her is just the kind of shit she doesn't want circulating around when she's trying to rebuild her life and repair the damage he did to her reputation."

"Are you and her...?" She let the question trail off but as her meaning sank in, he shook his head, adamant, not wanting her to get the wrong idea about him and Piper.

"*No*. Not at all, we're just friends, but he won't believe that. Simple truth is, he just can't face that this is all his doing. Always plays the victim, has to blame someone else."

She nodded, but he could tell from her expression that she didn't quite believe him and Wyatt felt strangely helpless when she released his hand. Then she raised a hand to gently brush her fingers over the left side of his face, her touch against his beard waking thousands of nerve endings as she looked at him with such concern that his hardened heart squeezed.

"You sure you're okay?" she asked softly.

"Yeah," he murmured, trying to remember why he shouldn't cup her face in his hands and taste that delectable mouth that had been tormenting him all night.

It had been so damn long since anyone had touched him this way, too long since he'd savored the feel of a woman's body beneath his, and the thought of feeling Austen's long limbs twine around him while he explored all that soft skin and found out what kinds of sounds she'd make while he pleasured her...

He shoved the tantalizing thought aside. "Much better now."

She gave him a soft smile that warmed him from the inside out, her fingertips lingering against his scruffy cheek. So gentle. So kind. "I'm glad." Humor sparkled in her silvery eyes. "Because you don't know how bad I wanted to pounce on him and beat the shit out of him for trying to hurt you."

Wyatt barked out a laugh, surprised and touched at the same time. "You know, I can totally see you doing it, too."

Her smile widened. "Dress, heels and all, I still pack quite a punch."

The humor faded. "I'm glad you didn't, though, since I would have felt compelled to stop you. Because I couldn't stand seeing you get hurt." Unable to resist the pull between them, he held her gaze as he turned his face and pressed his lips to her open palm.

She froze, her soft intake of breath sending a bolt of lust through him as her pupils expanded there in the glow of the porch light. Then she lowered her hand and the spell was broken, the singing of crickets filling the vacuum of silence.

"Well," she began, taking a step back and lowering her gaze. "It's getting late and we've both got an early start in the morning. I should probably go." She cocked her head. "Unless you want me to stick around to see if the cops want to question me as a witness?"

Hiding his disappointment, Wyatt shook his head. "It's okay." Probably for the best that she leave, considering how much he wanted her and how much he shouldn't touch her again.

It didn't matter that he liked and respected her. They'd almost crossed a line tonight and he couldn't risk it with them working together on this job for at least the next six months. It wasn't just him involved; his guys depended on the steady income this project would bring them. Signed contract with her or not, he couldn't risk screwing that up by sleeping with her and things turning awkward afterward.

Reminding himself of all that, he held the door for her while she went in to grab her purse, her scent wrapping around him as she walked past.

"I'll leave the list here for you," she said over her shoulder.

"Sure."

Holding Grits, wishing he was holding Austen instead, Wyatt mentally cursed as he watched her walk to her truck. Now he was even more pissed off at Greg. For the first time in forever he was actually interested in someone and now she thought there might be something going on between him and Piper, despite what he'd said.

God, he wished he'd punched that asshole in the face while he'd had the chance.

Chapter EIGHT

This wasn't even remotely the homecoming Easton had expected.

His first night home after another six-month stint in Afghanistan, he'd expected to hang out with his dad and Wyatt over some grilled steaks and cold beers. Instead he'd shown up to find his big brother wrestling with Greg on the cabin's front porch.

Greg's car was ahead of him now in the distance and it pissed Easton off that the guy was driving drunk. Easton had smelled the booze leaking out of his pores, and wasn't letting Greg out of his sight.

Especially not when Piper might be his next target.

He turned the corner sharply and hit the gas, racing to catch up with Greg's car so he wouldn't lose him. By now Wyatt would have called the cops, who were well acquainted with Greg Rutland and his bullshit. If he blew over the legal limit once they caught him, Greg would go to jail, and not even his former service as sheriff would make anyone down at the station or courthouse lift a finger to help him.

Up ahead, Greg turned a corner and disappeared from view into a subdivision just outside of town. Easton cursed and sped toward the intersection, his tires squealing as he made the turn thirty seconds later.

There were no taillights ahead of him on the darkened street.

Not about to give up, Easton turned onto each and every road in the residential area just south of downtown Sugar Hollow, searching for Greg's car. He found it a few minutes later, parked in the driveway of an unfamiliar one-story rancher.

Then he saw Greg standing on the front porch of the little bungalow arguing with someone, and Easton's stomach grabbed when he recognized the woman standing there in her robe.

Piper.

His hackles went up instantly, anger and protectiveness punching through him. "Oh, *hell* no." He'd always had a natural protective streak, but with Piper it was ten times as strong, because what he felt for her went way beyond friendship.

He roared up to the house and threw the truck into park at the curb, bursting out of it before it had stopped rocking. In three strides he was around the hood and heading for Greg, who'd half-turned to face him.

"Leave her alone," Easton warned, his eyes on Greg as he approached, ready for anything. Piper was standing there in front of her door, one hand clutching the lapels of her robe closed. The familiar weight of his pistol pressed against the small of his back but Easton wouldn't need it. If he had to take Greg down, he would do it with his bare hands.

Greg jutted his jaw out, his expression defiant. "We're not on your land anymore," he sneered, "and this is none of your business. Get back in your truck and get the hell out of here."

"Not a chance." He stormed up the front steps and stepped in front of Piper, reaching behind him with one hand to urge her back inside, his gaze locked on Greg. "Leave, now, before the cops get here and arrest your drunken ass. They're looking for you right now."

"You're just like your fucking arrogant brother," Greg snarled.

"I'll take that as a compliment."

"You would," he spat, pure hatred radiating from him.

"Greg," Piper said from behind him, sounding weary. "Just go. I've got nothing more to say to you."

Easton stood his ground, every cell in his body humming with the need to smash Greg's perfect teeth down his throat. If Greg wanted Piper, the asshole was going to have to go through him first. And Easton fought dirty. He'd served years in the Corps before joining the DEA and making it as a FAST operator.

Greg knew it, and the resignation in those deep blue eyes as they faced off told Easton he'd won for now. "The hell with both of you," Greg spat, and spun around to stalk to his car. A moment later the tires squealed as he peeled out of the driveway and took off, heading south.

Immediately Easton turned around to face Piper, seeming so small and fragile standing in her robe. She gasped when he took her by the shoulders and searched her face, her golden shoulder-length hair gleaming under the porch light. "Are you okay?"

"Yes," she said quietly, tugging the edges of her robe tighter around her body as she lowered her gaze.

"Did he threaten you?" If so, Easton would hunt him down and give him the beating he deserved.

Her shoulders moved in a tight shrug. "He's drunk."

"I don't fucking care, and don't make excuses for him. Did he threaten you?"

At the steel in his voice she met his gaze, and the pain and humiliation etched there hit him like a body blow. "I just want him to leave me alone," she whispered, her voice cracking.

Ah, hell. "I know, sweetheart." He pulled her into his arms, swallowing a groan at the feel of her as he pressed his nose to the top of her head, breathing in her shampoo and perfume.

He'd wanted to hold her like this for so damn long. More than a freaking decade, if he was honest. He'd hugged her plenty of times, but never held her this way. Offering comfort and solace and protection, the way a man held the woman he loved. It felt so damn good, even though he wished it wasn't happening because she was scared and embarrassed.

Piper sniffed and hitched in a choppy breath, on the verge of tears. "God, this is such a nightmare." She pushed at his chest and tipped her head back to meet his gaze, a frown pulling at her eyebrows. "How did you know he was coming here?"

"I followed him from Wyatt's place."

At that she blanched, her face losing all color. "What did he do now?" she demanded.

"Went over there looking for a fight. Something about how he can never measure up to Wyatt, and how he blames Wyatt for you leaving him."

She made a disgusted sound, her pretty hazel eyes narrowing to slits. "He's lost his mind."

Yeah, well, drugs did that to a person.

"Did he hurt Wyatt?"

"No, and by the time I jumped in, Wyatt already had him facedown on the porch."

She groaned, closed her eyes a second then opened them again. "Anyone else see?"

"Just me and Wyatt's date."

She stilled, her eyes widening. "His date? He had a date over?"

"Think so. Didn't recognize her."

"What did she look like?"

"Tall. Light brown skin, dark curly hair."

Another groan. "Austen."

"Who?"

"The woman who bought the Miller place. Wyatt's helping her fix it up."

Wait, the Miller place had sold? Damn…

"I'll call them both and apologize."

"No you won't. It's not your fault, it's his." She was putting on a brave front, but he could see she was trembling slightly. He rubbed his hands over her upper arms, trying to reassure and warm her, hating that her ex had the power to scare her so much. "Let's go inside. I think your neighbors have enough to gossip about already."

She allowed him to usher her inside and shut the door, then headed straight for the kitchen, where something delicious was baking. The house smelled like heaven, the scent of something sweet and tangy filling the air.

He glanced around the space, noting the stark contrast between the life of luxury she'd lived for the past six years as a Rutland, and the humble surroundings she found herself in now that she was back to being Piper Greenlee. Following her to the kitchen, he stood in the entryway and watched while she filled a kettle with water and set it on the stove.

"Smells good in here," he commented.

"Lemon bars, just out of the oven. Want one?"

"If you'll have one with me."

"Just one?" she said with a bitter laugh that set off warning bells. "Right. Because clearly I don't have self-control issues where fattening foods are concerned," she said, patting her hips.

Easton's gaze zeroed in on that area of her body, though the robe didn't exactly give him a good view. Yeah, she'd put on a little weight since he'd last seen her, but he thought it looked damn good on her. What would it feel like to wrap his hands around those lush hips, dig his fingers in to hold her still while he rode her? "Don't talk like that about yourself. You look great." Lush and womanly and edible in a way no man could fail to notice.

That was clearly the most inappropriate thing to be thinking about right now.

Frowning, he crossed his arms and leaned a shoulder against the wall. He'd had no idea things had gotten so bad between her and Greg. So he had to ask. "What the hell's happened around here in the six months I've been gone?"

Another laugh, the harsh edge to it making the back of his neck tingle. "*Shit* happened, Easton. And more of it keeps raining down on me every day." Her back was rigid as she moved around the kitchen, slicing the lemon bars and pulling out a teapot with her usual efficient manner. She was a one-woman powerhouse, always had been.

"You guys are separated, right?" That was the last he'd heard, from Wyatt, prior to his last deployment.

A stiff nod. "We're done. I'm just waiting for the one-year-mark to hit so I can file for divorce."

"He looks like he's really gone downhill lately." Greg had always had a substance abuse problem, but he'd been careful to hide it before. Easton hated the manipulative prick. It made him furious that the man had subjected Piper to that kind of life during their marriage. She deserved so much better. If she were Easton's, he would treat her like the goddess she was.

"Yeah, well, being an alcoholic and a drug addict on top of a manipulative liar will do that to a man. Eventually it catches up to you."

Easton was too stunned to reply. He'd known her marriage had been on the rocks before he'd left for Afghanistan last time, but no one had filled him in on the rest of it, or told him how bad things were. "I'm sorry. I didn't know." Why hadn't his family said anything to him?

Piper sighed, her shoulders sagging in the act of plating up a lemon square. "I asked your dad and Wyatt not to say anything. I didn't want anyone else to know how bad things had gotten."

That hurt. "Even me?"

Her eyes flashed up to his, full of sadness he would give anything to wipe away. "It wasn't personal. You know how it is around here. People were already whispering about it behind my back and I didn't want to add fuel to the gossip fires. I've been trying so hard to keep everything quiet, but when he goes out and does dickhead things like tonight, there's nothing I can do to limit the damage."

Easton crossed to the island in the center of the room and lowered himself onto one of the barstools across from where she stood. "Who cares what other people think of you? If they're stupid enough to lump you into the same category as him because of what he does, then that's their problem."

She gave him a wry look before reaching for a little sieve filled with powdered sugar. "You don't know me very well, do you?"

"I know you better than you think." And he so hated seeing her this way, sad, embarrassed, and hurting inside. He'd wanted her for so long, had been here all along and she'd never once seen him as anything but Wyatt's little brother. It was hard to take. He'd give anything to make her see him as a man, and the person who'd worshipped her for almost half his life.

"Here," she said, pushing a plate holding a powdered sugar-dusted lemon square and fork across the island.

He waited until she'd served herself one before taking a bite, and let out a groan at the perfect blend of sweet-tart that hit his tongue, the bright lemon flavor bursting on his taste buds. "Oh God, I fantasized about these while I was away."

Her lips quirked as she chewed. "Liar."

"No, I did. And your brownies and peach shortcake." And a lot of other things about her that he wouldn't mention. Most of them involving her being naked and under him.

"Well, in the last few months I've taken the baking thing to a whole new level." She stuffed another bite of lemon square into her mouth, and all he could do was stare at her lips as she chewed and imagine what they would feel like on his naked body.

He'd been carrying a torch for her since he was a teenager. It hadn't been a phase or just a crush. He'd hated that Wyatt had taken her to prom and dated her for a few weeks afterward. When they'd broken up it had been bittersweet because Easton no longer had to be jealous of his brother, but then the next day Wyatt had gone off to boot camp at Parris Island and nothing had been the same since.

Not that anyone knew about Easton's feelings for her. He had been careful to hide them from everyone, especially Piper. She'd been married, off limits.

She's not married anymore.

"I'm still really embarrassed that this happened, and that you felt the need to follow him tonight, but…" Her eyes flicked up to meet his. "I'm really glad you're here."

It took an act of will to stay where he was instead of rounding the island and pulling her into his arms so he could kiss her the way he'd been dying to all these years. But she was nowhere near ready for that, had no clue about his feelings for her, and he had to be patient. Break down her walls brick by brick, make her see that he was the one. The *only* one for her.

"Me too." His phone buzzed. He pulled it out to find a text from Wyatt.

You find him?

Yes, he answered. *I'm at Piper's place. He's gone now.* And he could well imagine the look on his brother's face when he read that news.

Asshole!!! Wyatt responded.

Major understatement.

Cops are out looking for him.

Keep me posted, Easton typed, then put his phone away. "That was Wyatt," he told Piper, answering the silent question in her eyes. "The cops are searching for Greg."

Her expression hardened and she looked down at her plate. "You probably wonder what I ever saw in him in the first place," she said softly.

"No. You saw what everyone else did at first, the image he wanted everyone to see." The decorated combat vet who'd been elected sheriff by his supporters, the son of a wealthy Virginia family that was willing to do anything and throw any amount of money out there to cover up whatever scandal Greg had created for himself. While dragging Piper along for the hellish ride on the downward spiral with him. "I just hate that you had to find out the truth about him the hard way."

She pressed her lips together. "Yeah. Me too. God, I feel like such an idiot. Everyone saw it but me. I've been holding off on serving him with a no-contact order, just to try and keep things quiet, but now I don't have a choice. Most of the time he's still coherent enough that I can talk him down, but tonight he was beyond that. He's been getting more and more unstable and I just can't risk it anymore."

Good girl. Except a no-contact order likely wasn't going to protect her if Greg decided to come after her again. He kept that to himself though. "I'm guessing this means his family's cut him off now? No more covering up his messes?" For people like the Rutlands, image was everything. Until even they had no choice but to recognize that the destructive path Greg had chosen had no end, and make the decision to cut him out of their lives.

She nodded. "They've cut him off completely, a couple months after I left him. That's when the real tailspin began."

There were so many things he wanted to ask her but he stayed silent, afraid he'd make her retreat when all he wanted her to do was lean on him more. Piper was proud and independent, and so damn sweet... She hadn't deserved any of this. "For the record? He didn't deserve you. Never did." *Sweetness, if you were mine...*

Before she could respond his phone buzzed again.

Cops arrested him for DUI. They're booking him right now.

Good, Easton replied. "They got him," he told Piper. "He'll be spending at least one night in jail."

At that a look of pure relief crossed her face and she let out a deep breath. "Thanks."

Had she been worried Greg might come back later, after Easton left? Had she been afraid he would hurt her? The questions made him crazy but he held them back, just wanting to give her what reassurance he could, make her feel safe.

"These lemon squares really are the best," he mumbled around another bite, his heart squeezing when a grateful smile broke across her face.

"I'm glad. It's nice to have someone to share them with for a change."

God, he couldn't stand the thought of her being lonely. He'd give his left arm to be able to pick her up and carry her back to her bedroom right now, strip that robe off her and worship her from head to toe. He'd pour his heart into making love to her, finally unveiling his feelings for her.

That's why he had to go. As much as he wanted to stay, he knew it was asking for trouble. She didn't realize what she meant to him and even if by some miracle she was lonely enough to turn to him right now in the moment, he wouldn't settle for a fling with her. Not ever.

He put their dishes in the dishwasher and crossed to her. Setting his hands on her shoulders, he looked down into her eyes. "Call me if you need anything, okay?" She had his number.

Another smile. "Thanks. I will."

After climbing behind the wheel of Wyatt's truck he waited until she turned out all the lights and sat there a moment. She was safe now. Greg would have to sleep it off overnight and would face charges in the morning. Hopefully, something would stick enough to land him some kind of punishment this time. Too often guys like him walked because of their past service and rich family.

His gaze cut to the window on the left when Piper raised the blind enough to peer out and wave at him, giving a thumbs-up and a grin that told him she'd known he would stand guard for a bit.

He waved goodnight, couldn't help the smile on his face or the sense of anticipation stirring in his gut. While he was sorry as hell for what she was going through, he was glad he'd been there for her tonight.

He drove away, lost in his thoughts. He didn't know if she'd ever return his feelings for her.

But at least now, for the first time ever, he finally had the chance to take a shot at making her his.

Chapter NINE

"All right, you stubborn bastard. It's on."

Shifting her stance, Austen raised the sledgehammer and slammed it into the upstairs bathroom countertop with all her might. The muscles and bones in her arms vibrated with the impact and she managed to punch a big hole in the top of the counter, but it still held firm to the wall.

She scowled and blew an errant curl away from her sweaty face. She'd only been at this for a few minutes already and she was about to melt up here. Damn vanity was freaking bombproof.

"Giving you a hard time?"

Her pulse jumped at the sound of that deep, sexy voice. She swung around to face Wyatt, standing outlined in the bathroom doorway.

Amusement danced in his eyes and he looked too delicious for words in his jeans and T-shirt that stretched across his muscular chest. It had been two days since the incident at his place with Piper's ex. Piper had called yesterday to apologize, and Austen had been quick to tell her it had nothing to do with her and wasn't her fault. Austen was more worried about Piper, to be honest.

"Yes, as a matter of fact." Wyatt had popped by earlier in the day to check on things, quiet and serious as ever as he went about his business and kept his guys on track, but then he'd left to help his dad at the farm. She hadn't expected him back so soon, but it was a nice surprise. "I don't know what the hell they built this thing with, but trust me when I say they just don't make 'em like this anymore."

Apart from the kitchen, gutting and expanding this bathroom was her biggest priority. She was sick of living at the motel and wanted to be able to stay here instead. Financially it didn't make sense for her to keep paying for a motel room when she could just as easily crash here once the plumbing and electrical systems were installed.

Wyatt eyed it, then her. "Want me to take a turn?"

Her back and arms ached and her hands were sore from wielding the sledgehammer. "Be my guest."

She handed it over and scooted back to rest one cheek on the edge of the claw foot tub she was determined to salvage, stripped off her work gloves and picked up the bottle of water that was now warm. Still, it was wet, and felt good on her dry throat, which got even drier as she watched Wyatt raise the sledgehammer and bring it down on the vanity.

Wood cracked and splintered under the force of the blow, and the edge of the counter came away from the wall a little. Everything feminine in her sighed and tingled at the blatant display of raw male power from such a tightly controlled man. What would it take to destroy that control?

She imagined stepping up behind him and pulling that shirt over his head, then sliding her hands up his ribs, over his chest and stomach. With his back to her she had no qualms about staring at the way the muscles in his arms and back flexed with each movement, or the way his jeans hugged his fine ass.

Over the past couple days, she'd thought a lot about that moment on his front porch after Piper's ex had driven off. It might have been a long time since she'd been interested in a man, but she recognized the signs when one was attracted to her and Wyatt definitely was.

Or at least, he had been.

Since the other night he'd kept a careful, professional distance from her. But she knew she hadn't imagined that leap of heat in his eyes when he'd stared down at her on his front porch. Watching him now, she was tempted to find out what would happen if she pushed him, stoked that hunger inside him.

Probably best if she avoided temptation, however, she thought as he continued dismantling the vanity blow by blow. They worked together and she depended on him and his crew to help her get this done. Despite his distant exterior he was solid and reliable and kept everyone on task, even her. If they hooked up and things went bad, it would be awkward. Maybe even awkward enough that they couldn't work together anymore.

She was curious about him though, wanted to know more about him and why he tended to avoid society. She liked him and could use a friend here…except she wanted to be more than his friend.

Part of her felt guilty for even thinking it, but John had been gone a long time and he wasn't coming back. He'd want her to move forward and get on with her life. He'd want her to be happy.

If Wyatt was to ask her out, she'd say yes without hesitation. She'd ask him out herself if she wasn't so afraid he'd turn her down flat. Would be nice if he did the pursuing though. Not that she'd hold her breath on that one.

Eight more blows from the sledgehammer and the countertop came away from the wall. "Think that did it," Wyatt announced, setting the hammer aside to look at her, barely breathing hard. "Gimme a hand?"

She jumped up, slipped on her gloves and grabbed the far end of the counter, the two of them yanking the framework away from the wall. One last pull and it came free, clattering to the floor…right on Wyatt's right boot.

"Oh!" Austen scrambled to her knees and grabbed it, tried to lug it off.

"No, it's—"

Ignoring him, she managed to pry it off his boot. When she looked up to check on him, Wyatt was grinning at her. She blinked. "Are you okay?"

He nodded. "No foot in there. Didn't feel a thing."

She flushed as his meaning sank in and floundered for a moment, trying to think of something to say. She couldn't believe she'd forgotten. But with him grinning at her like that, she couldn't help but laugh. "Okay, awkward moment over with, let's move on."

He held out a hand, palm up. She took it, allowed him to help pull her to her feet and the feel of that strong grip around her gloved hand sent another flutter through her. With them standing so close the bathroom suddenly seemed twice as small. And ten times as hot.

She lowered her gaze. "Thanks, I'll take this downstairs."

"I'll help you."

"No, I got it." Grabbing the countertop, she turned it sideways and tried to step by as she hefted it off the floor, her ass and shoulder blades rubbing against him as she squeezed past him and out into the hall.

God, the man was playing hell on her libido and she was pretty sure he had no idea. By the time these renos were done she might explode from unrequited desire and sexual frustration.

Lugging the counter through the front door, she heaved one end into the Dumpster before shoving the works into it. Just as she was dusting herself off, a car turned up the driveway. When the driver pulled up behind her truck and got out, alarm leapt inside her when she recognized Greg.

Her spine stiffened. She moved to the top of the stairs to bar him from coming any closer and put her hands on her hips. She wasn't going to let him go after Wyatt again.

Greg stopped at the bottom of the front steps and pulled off his sunglasses. "You Austen?"

She didn't answer verbally, just nodded. Why was he even out of jail?

"Is Wyatt inside?"

"He's busy." No way in hell she was allowing a repeat of the other night. "What do you want?"

He broke eye contact, glanced around the cluttered yard rather than look at her. "I wanted to apologize for the other night. I...wasn't myself."

Oh, from what she'd been told about him from two reliable sources since then, he'd been *exactly* himself the other night. "Anything else?"

He stared at her a moment, then shook his head. "No. Again, I'm sorry. If there's anything I can do, let me know."

You can get the hell off my property before Wyatt sees you, and not come back. Clearly he had issues, but part of her still wondered if there was any truth to his accusations about Wyatt and Piper. There was no denying they were close, and real fond of each other. "I'll tell him. Now leave."

Surprise flared in his eyes, as though he took offense at her ordering him off her property. Well, too bad. Her property, her rules. He could fucking deal.

To her relief he turned and headed for his car without another word, then got in and drove away. When he was halfway to the road, Wyatt came outside. A dark scowl lined his face as he stared after the retreating car. "What the hell did he want?"

"To apologize. I told him I'd pass on the message. As far as I can tell, he was sober."

Wyatt wrapped a hand around her upper arm and turned her to face him. The stark concern in his eyes sent a shiver of unease through her. "Stay away from him. I mean it. If he shows up here again, come get me and I'll handle it. If I'm not here, then call the cops. Don't talk to him again."

Concern for her safety was one thing, but she bristled at the blatant command in his voice. She wasn't one of his Marines to be ordered around. He wasn't a captain at her fire hall who got to tell her what to do and how to do it. She'd seen how Greg had behaved the other night. Just because she was a woman didn't mean she was weak and couldn't defend herself.

"I can look out for myself," she told him, a bite to her tone.

Jaw tight, he shook his head, his grip firm on her arm. "Not with him."

She jerked her arm free of his grasp and stepped back. Didn't matter that she knew he was worried about her. Nothing rankled her faster than someone bossing her around. "Okay, think I'm done for the day."

Turning away from him, she dug in her hip pocket for her keys and started down the steps to her truck.

"Austen."

Nope. She was tired and sweaty, pissed off by his heavy-handed attitude, and increasingly sexually frustrated by just being near him. She needed to get away from him for a while. A long cool shower followed by a cold drink and a nap sounded a lot more preferable to sticking around here with him.

"Text me if you need me to answer anything," she threw over her shoulder, not even bothering to look at him as she got in her truck and drove to her motel.

****

Standing outside the second floor motel room door, Wyatt resisted the urge to fidget as he waited for Austen to answer. It had been five hours since she'd jumped in her truck and driven away from the jobsite. He'd thought about texting her rather than just showing up here but even he knew that wasn't going to clear the air between them.

When he'd seen Greg's car driving down her driveway he'd reacted without thinking, only worried about her safety because he knew what a piece of shit Greg was, and what he was capable of when he was wasted. He hadn't meant to sound overbearing and domineering, but he guessed he had.

The door swung open and Austen stood there with an unreadable expression on her face and wearing a red wrap-around dress that hugged every curve of her long, lean body, the low neckline displaying the tops of her breasts.

Tearing his gaze from her cleavage, he met her cool stare. "I came to apologize," he blurted, thrusting the bouquet of flowers he'd bought at her.

She took them, lowered her head to smell them even as she held eye contact. For some reason he found that direct gaze sexy as hell. "Wow, that's two men who've apologized to me in the space of a few hours. Not sure that's ever happened before."

He couldn't tell if she was still pissed at him or not. "But mine was better, right? More sincere."

She nodded, one side of her mouth curving upward. Okay, she couldn't be *too* mad if she was smiling. "And you brought flowers. So yes, yours is better."

"So…I'm forgiven?" He wanted to make sure. Sometimes with women, he couldn't tell.

She gave him a considering look. "Mostly."

He frowned. "If I took you to dinner, would that do it?"

Her eyebrows went up. "It might. Couldn't hurt to try it, anyway."

Damn, he was torn between wanting to squirm and pulling her into his arms to kiss her until she couldn't stand up on her own. "Can we go tonight?" It was already after six. The woman had to eat sooner or later.

"We could," she hedged. "What did you have in mind?"

"There's a place on the river I'd like to take you to."

She straightened, cocked her head. "Is this a date?"

"No," he said quickly, because that would be totally inappropriate. She was his boss. Well, technically she was, according to their contract. Didn't matter, because right now he was all about inventing excuses to help him maintain his distance from her.

"No?" She lifted a dark eyebrow.

He could feel the heat rushing into his cheeks and was grateful that his beard would hide most of it. Wait. "Do you want it to be?"

"Do you?"

Shit, he didn't know what to say to that. He was so far off his game it wasn't even funny. He'd been out of the dating scene for a long time and Austen threw all the rules he'd thought he'd known completely out the window. He was off balance and flailing. "We work together."

"We do," she agreed, then grinned. "Doesn't have to be a date. But I wouldn't mind if it was."

Damn. He hadn't been prepared for that one, or the rush of desire her words triggered.

She let out a light laugh. "You're so cute when you get flustered."

Flustered? He frowned. "I'm not flustered."

"Sure." Her grin widened. "Are you driving?"

Sure as hell didn't feel like it at the moment. "Uh, yeah."

"I'll be down in two minutes." Shooting him a mysterious smile that made him want to follow her inside and press that luscious body against the wall so he could feel her as he kissed her breathless, she shut the door in his face.

He'd barely pivoted on his heel when his cell dinged with an incoming text from another number he didn't recognize.

What are you most afraid of?

His pulse skipped. The asshole was back.

Another ding. *I'm going to take away the thing you love.*

All right, who the fuck was this? Frustration pulsed through him as he tightened his grip on the phone.

That red dress is so sexy on her. Your girl is hot. I think I'd like to feel her from the inside out.

Wyatt's blood chilled. His head snapped up, his gaze automatically scanning the parking lot and surrounding area. Whoever sent the texts had seen them just now.

He didn't see anyone. This being a parking lot, there were plenty of places for someone to hide. *Dammit.*

He scowled. *Fuck you, asshole*. He dialed Charlie as he stalked toward his truck, keeping an eye on Austen's door just in case.

"Hey, you," his sister answered. "How are things?"

"My psycho stalker just upped his game," he answered. "He was watching me as of a few minutes ago."

Charlie sucked in a sharp breath. "Did you see him?"

"No, but he saw me and the woman I was just talking with. He mentioned the color of her dress to let me know." Now he was worried about her.

"What the hell? Who would be playing with you like that?"

"Not a freaking clue. Can you help?"

"Sure, send me screenshots of the texts and the number they came from. I'll have my guys run the number when they get a chance. Might not be for a few hours." She paused. "I hate to be a downer, but you know it's probably another disposable phone, right?"

"Yeah," he ground out, checking around him again. If he got lucky, the guy had paid for it by credit card and Charlie would be able to trace it. God, it pissed him off that anyone would threaten him, but even more that someone would threaten Austen. He shouldn't have to watch his back here at home, where he was supposed to be safe again, and neither should she. "Call me if you find out anything, okay?" Austen was just coming down the stairs, looking delectable in that sexy red dress.

"I will. Be careful."

"Roger that. Bye, Charles." Tucking his phone away, he slid out to give Austen a smile as he opened her door for her.

Chapter TEN

The restaurant Wyatt chose was beautiful, in an old heritage house set right on the river. Austen eyed him over the top of her wineglass as he perused his menu. He might not want to call this a date, but it sure as hell felt like one to her. A cozy table for two at the back of the restaurant next to the window, candlelight, wine. Romantic.

He glanced up from his menu, those gorgeous hazel eyes connecting with hers. "See anything you like?"

Oh yeah, several things, only they weren't on the menu. "Food looks great."

He set his menu down. "We can go someplace else if you'd rather." He glanced around once before looking back at her. "I thought you'd like it."

She knew he was uncomfortable enough going out in public, let alone to a new place. He seemed a little stiff, even for him, and she wondered if it was because it made him uncomfortable for strangers to see his scars. It hadn't escaped her notice that he'd seated himself with the scarred side of his face toward the window, where no one could see it.

"Would you rather go somewhere else instead?" she asked.

"No, it's fine. But I should have warned you that by morning rumors will have spread all over town that we were here together."

She shrugged. "I don't care what people say. I'm done with worrying about what others think of me and my decisions."

He looked down at the candle burning between them. "Sorry, I'm not great about being out in public. I hate the stares and the whispers. Makes me feel like a freak of nature."

She hadn't thought he'd be that self-conscious—he seemed so confident and alpha all the time, it hadn't even occurred to her, and now she felt bad for putting him in this position. She glanced around them, spotted a couple people looking at him. "We could order something to go then take a drive and eat in your truck."

"No, it's okay." He was clearly making an effort for her sake and while she appreciated it, she didn't want to make him uncomfortable. "Just glad they don't bother you."

"Honestly I don't even notice them anymore."

He met her gaze, his eyes assessing, then glanced away.

She toyed with the stem of her wineglass. "How did it happen?" she asked softly.

He stilled, his jaw clenching, and just when she was sure he wouldn't answer, he spoke. "On patrol in Afghanistan. We got into a tight spot."

She waited, not saying anything.

"I was leading my squad and we walked into an ambush. When the shooting started, I missed an IED alert."

"Raider."

He nodded. "She was trained to alert me to explosives by sitting. I had her leash attached to my belt but with everything going on my attention was divided. By the time I realized what she was trying to tell me, it was too late."

Part of her felt like she should change the subject, but another part was worried that if she tried, he'd feel like she was trivializing or brushing off what had happened. "But they got you out."

"Yeah." He leaned back in his chair. "I was pretty out of it. I lost consciousness on the flight back to Kandahar. My next clear memory is waking up in Germany with my brother, Brody, standing next to my bed."

"I'm glad he was there for you."

"They all were. My dad, Easton, and my sister, Charlie, were all waiting for me when I landed in D.C. One of them stayed with me every single day through those first three months." A smile tugged at his mouth. "No matter how much of a pain in the ass I was or how hard I pushed them away, they always stayed." His eyes held a faraway look. "I'll never forget that."

After a moment his eyes cleared and he focused on her. "That's partly why I was such an asshole to you the day we met."

"Oh?"

"I'd just come from a...family situation and I was still pretty upset. I'd barely walked in the door when Piper called to tell me you'd bought the house."

She winced. "Wow. Sorry." Though she was curious about what he meant by "family situation", she decided it was best not to ask.

"I'm not making excuses for the way I acted. Just wanted to explain. You close to your family?"

"Just my mom, although I don't see her as much as I'd like. My dad left us when I was just a baby and she remarried when I was in my teens. She lives in Mississippi with my stepdad, who's not my favorite person, but at least he treats her well." She sipped her wine. "I'm still close with John's sister and parents. They live up in Philly and I talk to them a few times a week. They hate that I moved away, but I just really needed the space to start fresh."

He nodded. "I can understand that."

"What's the deal with you and Piper, anyway?"

He blinked at her. "What do you mean?"

"I can tell you're pretty close, and she obviously cares about you a lot. And then the other night Greg said…"

His expression hardened. "Greg is a lying, manipulative bastard, and on top of that he's a drunk and a cokehead. Don't listen to a thing he says."

"So why did he think she's still hung up on you?"

He shrugged. "He's looking for excuses so he doesn't have to face the guy in the mirror and admit why she walked out. Piper and I are old friends, and that's it. We dated after senior prom for a couple weeks, and we broke up when I left for boot camp. But my family loves her, and as far as we're concerned, she's one of us. Anyone messes with her, they mess with all of us."

Austen smiled, loving the show of protectiveness. "So she's got three badass former Marine brothers to watch her back."

"Four, including my dad," he said with a smile. "But seriously, there's nothing going on between us."

Okay, that made her feel a lot better.

"Wyatt."

They both turned in their seats as Scott wove his way between the tables toward them. A tiny prick of alarm jumped inside her. This place was a ways out of town. Had he followed them here?

"Hey." Wyatt stood and shook his hand. "What are you doing here?"

"I was driving past and saw your truck out front. You not coming to the range tonight?"

"No, I've got plans." He smiled at her.

Scott's gaze shifted to her and something in his eyes that she couldn't put a finger on sent a thread of unease down her spine. Then he nodded at her in polite acknowledgment before he looked back at Wyatt, and the feeling disappeared. "Oh. That's too bad, the guys and I were looking forward to putting some rounds downrange with you."

"Next time."

An awkward beat of silence passed between them, then Scott put on a smile. "Okay. Well, have a good night." His gaze slid to her for a moment before he walked away.

Austen held off on asking Wyatt about Scott's story because the server arrived with their meals. They ate and talked some more, getting to know each other better. He liked military thrillers and country music, while she preferred romantic comedies and pop songs. He loved to ride horses and shoot, and she liked to fish and play basketball.

"You like to fish?" Wyatt asked, staring at her in astonishment.

"Love it. I'm pretty good at it too."

He settled back into his seat. "Huh. Maybe we can go fishing together sometime."

"Sure, if you don't mind me coming home with all the big ones."

He grinned, and it completely transformed the harsh planes of his face. Her heart fluttered, the slow burn of arousal firing her blood.

"Was it hard, being a firefighter?" he asked after the server cleared their plates.

"Sometimes. Any calls involving kids were the hardest. Some of the accidents we responded to really stayed with me. And when you just knew the outcome wasn't going to be good…yeah, that was tough."

He nodded, and she knew he understood because he'd been in combat. Not the same thing, but similar in some ways. "You want dessert?"

Oh, man, do I. In the form of a six-foot-plus, gruff and sexy man sitting across from me. "I couldn't eat another bite."

He paid the bill and walked her to his truck, opened and shut her door for her before climbing behind the wheel.

"What's the deal with Scott, anyway?" she finally asked as he drove.

"He suffered a TBI in Afghanistan about eighteen months ago. Why?"

"I dunno. Sometimes he and Eddie—well, more Eddie—make me a little uncomfortable."

Wyatt shot her a frown, a subtle tension taking root in his posture. "Why, have either of them done or said something to you?"

"No. Just a feeling I get." She waved a hand. "Maybe I'm just being paranoid."

"You should have told me. I'll talk to them both."

"*No*, don't." That wouldn't make things better; she just wanted to let him know about her intuition. "I'll let you know if anything bothers me going forward."

He eyed her, raised an eyebrow. "Promise? Because I'll handle it if it does."

"Promise."

Wyatt was quiet for a long moment. "They're decent guys who've been through a lot. Both of them lost their battle buddies over there, along with other friends. All the guys on the crew had a tough time after coming home, can't seem to fit back into society anymore." He grunted. "I hire them because I know exactly what that feels like."

She looked over at him, admiring the strong lines of his profile. "You seem to have adjusted really well, all things considered."

He made a face. "I'm better than I was, but I'll never be the same. That's the hardest part, other than the people we lose when we go to war. Knowing you don't belong anymore when you come back home."

"Because of survivor's guilt?"

He nodded once. "Partly. More like you don't have anything in common with anyone all of a sudden. Like, we've been overseas fighting for our lives and losing people and people here are more concerned about what's going on in reality TV."

Now it was her turn to make a face. "Yeah, that would be hard. And insulting."

He grunted in agreement. "I'll keep my eye on the guys, but seriously, if anything comes up, just tell me and I'll handle it."

His tone made it clear he was willing to pull them off the job if she wanted. She hoped it wouldn't come to that. "I will. Thanks."

He cleared this throat, shifted in his seat. "There's...something else I need to tell you."

At his grim tone, she looked sharply at him. "What's that?"

"I've been getting these weird texts over the past couple days. I don't know who's sending them."

This didn't sound promising. "What kind of texts?"

"Threats."

Her eyebrows shot up. "For real?"

He nodded once, appearing uncomfortable. "My sister is an analyst with the DEA. She's tracing the numbers the calls have come from, but so far she can't find anything to ID the person. And then tonight, before we left the motel, I got another one. It mentioned you."

Cold spread through her gut. "What did it say?"

"It mentioned your red dress. Whoever it was saw us."

She shook her head as she leaned back against the leather seat. "You should have told me."

"I…yeah. I should have." He rubbed a hand over the back of his neck. "Sorry."

Pulling in a slow breath, she ordered herself to stay calm. "Anything else?"

He seemed to hesitate a moment before replying, and she knew he was withholding something from her. "He just wanted me to know he saw us together."

Yeah, and that bothered her. "What does he want?" Assuming it was a he.

"To piss me off, or maybe scare me. Not sure."

"And you don't have any idea who it is?"

He shook his head. "None. I don't want you to worry, I just thought you had a right to know."

She wished he'd done it right away, rather than wait, but decided to let it go. "Okay."

At her motel he walked her up to her door. Touched by the show of manners, she smiled up at him. "Thanks for dinner. I enjoyed it."

"Me too."

She hid a smile, angled her body to face him and took a step closer, enjoying that they were eye to eye. "So, did this qualify as a date?"

"I…"

"Because if it did, then you need to kiss me goodnight."

For a moment, Wyatt was too stunned to answer her.

A heady shot of arousal punched through him, momentarily scrambling his brain. There were so many reasons why he shouldn't touch her, but at the moment none of them seemed important enough to keep his hands off her.

Without giving himself time to overthink it he stepped forward, erasing the distance between them, and slid one hand into those springy curls he'd been wanting to touch. She leaned toward him, eyelids falling closed and he took the invitation, settling his mouth over hers.

The moment their lips touched a rush of desire swept through him. Her hands came up to settle on his chest and she leaned closer.

Wyatt kissed the corner of her mouth, her bottom lip, then grazed his tongue along it. She made a soft sound in the back of her throat and curled her fingers into his shoulders as she opened for him.

He delved inside her, stroked her tongue with his. She moaned into his mouth and the kiss changed instantly.

Bringing his other hand up to cup the back of her neck, he pushed her backward and pressed her up against the door. Austen shivered lightly and slid her hands up to grip his head, arching to bring their bodies in contact from chest to groin.

He was already hard and aching and wanted her to feel what she did to him. He pressed his erection into the softness of her lower belly, amazed at how well they fit together. It was like she was built for him.

Rubbing against her, reveling in the tiny catch in her breathing and the light shiver that rippled through her, he flicked his tongue against hers and teased the roof of her mouth. She wrapped one long leg around his thigh and rocked into him, damn near making his eyes roll into the back of his head.

He hadn't been with anyone since being injured. If things progressed between them—and this mind-blowing kiss suggested that they would—then she would wind up seeing *all* of him.

The thought sent a trickle of unease through him. She seemed strong and calm and accepting but a beautiful woman like her could do so much better than a mentally and physically scarred guy like him.

He knew what he looked like, and it wasn't pretty. Part of him couldn't believe she'd actually wanted him to kiss her, let alone how into it she seemed.

Wanting to stop things before they got out of hand, he drew her lower lip into his mouth and sucked lightly, flicking the tip of his tongue against it before raising his head. She made a sound of protest and tried to lean in for more but he eased back, his grip firm on her nape.

Dazed silver eyes slowly focused on his face as she blinked up at him. He couldn't help but smile. "Wow."

A lazy, seductive smile curved her shiny lips. "Wow is right." Her hands gentled on his head, her fingers stroking over his scalp in a way that sent little shivers over his skin. "I haven't kissed anyone like that since John, and I can definitely say that was worth the wait."

Yeah? Then they had more in common than he'd realized.

Despite their poor beginning, things were good between them now. He was comfortable around her, enjoyed her company. He wished he was still kissing her, or better yet, backing her into the motel room and slowly stripping her clothes off to reveal every inch of her smooth brown skin so he could stroke and taste it.

"For me, too," he said.

Her gaze dropped to his mouth again, then came back to his eyes. It had been a damn long time since he'd been with a woman but even he couldn't mistake the hunger burning in her eyes. For a second he was sure she was going to invite him inside, but then she touched her lips to his in a light caress and released his head.

"Thanks for tonight, I enjoyed it. Have a good night."

Torn between relief and disappointment, he eased his fingers from her curls and released the back of her neck. "You too."

She shot one last seductive smile at him before slipping into the room and shutting the door.

The moment he turned around he saw the car parked at the rear of the lot. Unease filled him as soon as the driver saw him watching. Before he could move or make out who the driver was, the person turned their head to face front and hit the gas, tearing out of the lot, too fast for Wyatt to see the plate but he got the make and model.

A warning tingle in his gut told him it hadn't been coincidence. That the driver had been watching him and Austen, had been sitting there watching them kiss. And they still hadn't found out who had sent him those texts. Whoever it was might be following him around, maybe targeting Austen.

His mind went back to what Austen had said at dinner. It could have been Greg, but what if it was one of the guys on his crew?

His immediate reaction was to dismiss that any of the guys were behind this, because he knew them all personally and there was no reason for any of them to target him. Hell, he'd gone out of his way to provide them with enough work to support themselves.

Those texts though... They had to be from someone he knew. Or someone Austen knew.

God, he hated that she was alone at this motel. It might be nothing and he might just be acting paranoid, but what if the driver had been watching Austen and waiting for Wyatt to leave so he could make a move?

Not wanting to worry her further by telling her about the car in case he was being paranoid, he pulled out his phone to dial Easton.

"Hey," his brother said. "You didn't show up for dinner. Had a last minute hot date or something?"

"Something came up."

"Wait, what? Was it a date?" A pause, and he imagined his brother's wide-eyed expression. "Is it the girl you invited over for dinner?"

He wasn't touching that one with a ten-foot pole because if he did, Easton would badger him forever. Literally. Forever. "I need a favor."

"Oh. Sure, man. What's up?"

"I need you to meet me at the motel off Main and switch vehicles with me."

"You took your date back to a *motel*? Jesus, Wyatt, I know it's been a while since you were in the saddle, but—"

"It's not like that," he snapped, impatient. "Look, can you come switch vehicles with me or not?"

"Yeah, sure. Be there in twenty."

Wyatt ended the call and stood beside his truck, keeping an eye out for that gray car, but it didn't come back. Easton pulled into the parking lot right on time and parked beside him. "Hey. Everything okay?"

He sighed. "Someone's watching me. Or maybe Austen."

"Austen? The girl from last night?"

He nodded. "She bought the Miller place and is fixing it up."

"Dad told me." He frowned. "You think someone is after her?"

"No." *Maybe.* "I don't know. She's new in town so it's unlikely she's had time to make any enemies here, and I can't see anyone not liking her anyhow." Though he didn't know much about her past, so he couldn't rule out the possibility that someone was targeting her. But then why text him instead of her?

He told Easton about the texts, and of course Easton already knew about Greg. Then he explained about the car and driver, and shrugged. "Might be nothing, but I still don't know who sent me those texts so I'd feel better if I camped outside for tonight, see if they come back."

Easton blinked at him, then a shit-eating grin split his face. "You're really into her. Austen."

Wyatt didn't answer for a moment. "I just want to make sure she's safe."

His brother wiped the grin off his face and nodded, but Wyatt could still see the amusement glinting in those brown eyes. "Sure, bro, you gotta do what you gotta do. Here." He held up a set of keys and swapped with Wyatt. "I left your present on the passenger seat. Was going to give it to you last night, but you were otherwise…occupied, so…" He thumped Wyatt on the shoulder. "Happy belated birthday."

"Thanks, man."

"See you tomorrow? Maybe we can grab breakfast or something before you head to work."

"Sounds good. Can you look after Grits for me?"

"I brought him in my truck. I fed and walked with him so he's got a full belly and he's all empty down below. Cute little guy."

"Yeah." He was growing on Wyatt more and more every day, making it hard to keep his emotional distance. Piper was no doubt gloating about what an awesome idea it had been to give the dog to him in the first place. "Thanks, man. Later."

"Later." Easton climbed into Wyatt's truck.

Wyatt watched his brother drive away. It had been way too long since they'd all been together, with Easton being overseas for six months at a time and Brody recovering from a bullet wound that could have ended his career on the HRT. Charlie's schedule as a DEA computer forensic examiner was erratic too. This past year they hadn't even celebrated Christmas together. Their mother must have rolled over in her grave.

His gaze strayed to the upper floor of the motel, to Austen's door. His mom would have loved her. What was Austen doing right now? Was she in the shower, standing under the flow of hot water as it slid over her lithe, naked body?

He caught his breath. Was she in bed, thinking of him? Better yet, was she touching herself, to ease the ache that kiss had ignited? Because he was sure as hell aching for her.

It blew him away that he wanted her this badly, more than he'd ever wanted another woman, and that she'd managed to get under his skin in such a short time, let alone after the bad start they'd had.

Pushing out a deep breath to banish the images those thoughts created, he got into Easton's truck and greeted Grits with an ear-ruffle. A rolled-up T-shirt sat on the passenger seat. Wyatt picked it up and unrolled it.

When he read the message on the front, he couldn't stop the crack of laughter that escaped. His little brother was awesome.

After putting it on, he drove around the block, looking for the gray car. When he didn't see it, he parked at the far end of the parking lot and shut off the engine, leaned the seat back.

It was going to be a long and fairly uncomfortable night, but he didn't sleep much these days anyway and he just wanted to make sure Austen was safe.

Chapter ELEVEN

Dressed in her workout gear of yoga pants and a sports top, Austen crossed the parking lot, headed for the sidewalk that would take her to Main Street. She stuffed her hands in her pockets to ward off the chill of the early morning air.

It was just after five, and chilly. After suffering a long night filled with sexual frustration that even her favorite battery-operated toy couldn't completely alleviate, she was sorely in need of a serious caffeine jolt and had woken up with the worst craving for one of the *Garden of Eatin'*'s vanilla lattes.

Nearly to the sidewalk, she did a double-take at the man asleep behind the wheel of a white pickup. Wyatt?

She started toward him, taking in the way his head lolled back against the headrest. When she drew nearer she saw that his mouth was partially open, his chest rising and falling in an even rhythm. What the hell was he doing here, asleep in a strange truck?

Standing directly beside his window, she lifted a hand and gently tapped on it. He jerked awake like she'd fired a gun, his frantic gaze calming only when he focused on her standing there.

"Hey," he mumbled, reaching up to grimace and rub the back of his neck.

"What are you doing sleeping out here?" she asked.

He rolled down the window and Grits climbed over the top of him to stick his head through the window, trying to lick her. She patted him while she waited for Wyatt's response.

"Long story," he said, and frowned. "What time is it?"

"Ten after five. Wyatt." His sleep-bleary eyes focused on her. "Why did you stay here in this truck last night?"

"I thought I saw someone watching me after you went inside. They were in a car at the back of the parking lot and took off when I saw them." He shrugged, the motion tight, almost defensive. "After those texts, I didn't want you to be here alone, just in case."

She melted a little. "You could have just come up to my room."

He snorted. "Not a good idea."

She thought it would have been one hell of an idea.

His frown deepened. "What are you doing up and dressed already?"

"Couldn't sleep so I thought I'd wander down to the café for the biggest latte they can make me." Withdrawing her hand from Grits's head, she folded her arms and gave Wyatt a stern look. "Whose truck is this?"

"My brother Easton's. He came and traded vehicles with me."

"And you stayed out here all night because of that car?" There had to be more to it.

116

He lifted a shoulder. "I learned in Afghanistan not to ignore my gut, so I couldn't leave last night. Wanted to make sure you were safe."

Her heart turned over. She couldn't believe he'd spent the entire night like that, his huge frame squished into the front seat. He must be stiff and sore, sitting up like that for so long, and she doubted he'd slept even as well as she had when she'd managed to doze off. All because he'd wanted to guard her.

God, he was such a complex man. Hard in a lot of ways, and soft in so many others. She never knew what to expect from him.

She sighed. "You remember I was a firefighter, right? And I'm a pretty big girl, in case you haven't noticed. I wouldn't make for an easy target. I'm not helpless."

"I know. I just…I felt like I needed to stand watch."

Awww. She eyed him for a long moment. "Feel like an early morning walk? I owe you a coffee at the very least."

"You don't owe me anything. But I'll go with you if you want the company."

"I do." She stepped back to let him get out, accepted Grits's leash when Wyatt handed it to her. The little dog jumped down and scampered up to her feet, his tail going a hundred miles an hour. "You're a morning person, huh?" she asked him, giving his head a scratch.

"You have no idea," Wyatt muttered as he got out and stretched his arms over his head, bringing her attention to the way his muscles flexed. And when she saw what was written on the front of his T-shirt, she couldn't help the shocked laugh that escaped her.

I had a blast in Afghanistan.

Another laugh burst out of her. Really? It seemed so unlike him. "Huh. So you do have a sense of humor after all," she teased.

"Guess so," he said with a grin that did funny things to her insides. "Easton gave it to me last night."

"I like it."

"Yeah, me too. Ready?"

For? She'd lost her train of thought completely because she'd been gazing into his eyes. "Yes." She held Grits's leash as they walked down Main Street toward the café. The dog trotted a little in front of her, pulling to the side whenever he smelled something interesting.

"Who's walking who there?" Wyatt asked, amusement in his voice.

She looked over at him, surprised. "What?"

He shook his head, a grin playing around his mouth. "You gotta show him who's boss."

Fine. She shortened the leash and gave a sharp tug. "Grits. Heel."

The dog glanced back at her, ears perked, then faced forward and carried on exactly as before. Austen shot him an annoyed look. *Buddy, you're making me look bad.*

"So, get any sleep last night?" she asked Wyatt casually.

"Yeah, some." He glanced at her. "You?"

"Same. Guess I was feeling…restless."

At that his eyes heated, and the hunger there was ten times as powerful to her because he was always so contained. She'd be lying if she didn't admit she'd wondered what he'd be like in bed, whether he'd be controlled or whether he'd let the leash slip on his need. She mentally bit her lip as something low in her abdomen fluttered.

"You know where to find me if you want to take care of that." His voice was low, sexy as hell.

Oh, so it was going to be like that, was it? He was waiting for her to drop the hammer and make the next move?

118

It threw her. In the past, the men she'd dated—even John—had always been the pursuer. That was her comfort zone, to sit back and let them woo her. But she had to admit, the prospect of seducing Wyatt was surprisingly hot.

Various scenarios played in her mind as they walked to the café. Surprising him at the cabin while he was asleep seemed pretty damn sexy. She'd crawl under the sheets beside him and stop his question with a slow, deep kiss, then explore him from head to toe, learning what made him suck in his breath and what made him moan.

She'd bet he slept naked. Starkly, gloriously naked, those lucky sheets caressing his warm, bare skin.

She was prevented from making a witty comeback because her brain had suddenly ceased to function, and another couple was walking their dog toward them. Grits went all giddy, hopping on his hind legs and whimpering, tail a blur of motion.

Austen gave him more leash and let him go up to sniff the lab mix. They did the whole butt-sniffing thing and started moving in a circle, getting their leads tangled in the process.

"Aw, he's so sweet," the other woman said, bending to pet Grits. "How old is he?"

"Two," Wyatt answered, standing there like a proud papa as he watched Grits interact with the other dog.

Austen couldn't contain her snicker as they began walking away. "Nah, you're not attached to him at *all*."

He gave an easy shrug, a half-grin on his face. "What can I say, he's growing on me."

At the café they ordered a giant latte for her and a large black coffee for him, along with some pastries, then sat at a table out back on a pretty brick patio covered by a pergola. The wisteria growing on it was in

119

full bloom, scenting the air with its sweet fragrance and dropping lavender petals on the rust-red bricks.

A few minutes into their breakfast he glanced up to find her watching him, and raised an eyebrow.

She shook her head once and wrapped her hands around her warm mug. "I didn't see you coming, Wyatt. When I moved here, the last thing I expected was to become interested in someone."

"Is that what you are? Interested?"

"Extremely interested. I'm not the only one, right?"

The look he gave her over top of the rim of his mug made her toes curl in her trainers. "You couldn't tell while I was kissing you last night?"

Oh, his voice while he said it, all low and gravelly. It made her insides melt. "Just wanted to confirm. And now you've had a night to sleep on it. Still haven't changed your mind?"

His gaze heated, and his expression turned lazy as he stared back at her. She was dying to know what it would be like with him in bed. "Nope."

A grin tugged at her mouth. "Good."

A few other people trickled out to join them, so they kept the conversation neutral for the rest of their visit. But all the while, tingles of excitement fizzed in her stomach like the finest champagne.

Afterward they walked back to her motel. He was vigilant, but not on guard and being next to him made her feel safe. "Any word on who might have sent you those texts?" she asked.

"None. Whoever it is must be using burner phones. He or she was in the area, but I don't have a name."

She stopped in front of her door. It was adorable to see such a big man walking a toy breed. Piper was right about his big heart underneath that alpha exterior.

Without giving herself time to overthink it, she cupped the side of his face with one hand and leaned in to cover his lips with hers. He made a low sound in the back of his throat that made her core clench and slipped a hand into her hair, cradling her head in his palm as he kissed and teased and stroked until her legs began to feel weak.

When he lifted his head a minute later she was breathless, one hand braced on his solid chest. She could feel his heart thudding beneath her palm, sure and steady.

She rubbed her hand over the spot, smiled up at him. "See you at work in a little while?"

Hunger burned in his eyes. "You can count on it, sweetheart."

The endearment sent a wave of heat through her body. She locked the motel room door behind her, hoping she could count on a whole lot more from him later on tonight. Maybe even the start of something wonderful.

****

Late that afternoon Austen was busy working on the kitchen cabinets she'd built. To match the existing woodwork scattered elsewhere throughout the room, she'd decided to add embellishments like scrollwork and fleurs-de-lis on some of the trim.

She paused when she spotted Wyatt in her peripheral vision. Shutting off the sander, she pushed her goggles to the top of her head and faced him. "Hey."

"You're making good progress," he said, inspecting what she'd accomplished so far.

"Sort of. Not nearly as fast as I'd like though." She checked her watch then glanced back at him. "You taking off?"

"Yeah, have to take my dad in for another appointment. You okay here without me? A couple of the guys are still working but Eddie and Scott just left."

"Yeah, I'm good." The way Wyatt was willing to step up and help his father made her admire him all the more. "See you in the morning then?"

He hesitated, and she could tell he didn't want to leave. Was he worried about her safety? She was perfectly safe here. "Want to come out to the house for dinner tonight? My brother Easton will be there, and maybe my sister, if she can make it. If you're not comfortable with it, though, I understand."

The offer took her by surprise. Wyatt was a private person. "No, I'd love to come. Can I bring anything?"

He shook his head. "Nah, we'll handle it. Around seven?"

"Sure, sounds good."

As he turned and walked away she admired the way he moved. Solid, confident, a man who knew who he was and what he wanted. So sexy.

She finished sanding everything down and was getting ready to glue the embellishments onto one of the cabinets when movement to her right caught her eye.

Pausing, she was startled to find Piper standing there. A saw whined upstairs, the smell of sawdust thick in the air. "Hey, you finally came to check the place out."

"I couldn't resist," Piper said, grinning at her before gazing around the gutted kitchen. "Wow, sure looks different in here."

"Yeah. Right now we're in that ugly in-between phase where everything looks a whole lot worse before it'll start looking better."

Piper held up a familiar pink bag. "Brought you something. Can you take a break?"

"Sure can." She eyed the bag with interest. "What'd you bring?"

"You'll just have to wait and see." She angled her head toward the rear doors that led from the kitchen out onto the back deck. "Care to eat outside?"

Austen led the way out onto the deck where she'd placed the plastic folding chairs she'd bought at the hardware store. "Have a seat."

Piper sank into one of them and stretched her legs out in front of her, the frayed cuffs of her jean shorts stopping halfway up her thighs. Her toenails were a bright, shocking pink and a delicate gold chain wrapped around her ankle. Birds chirped in the trees and a hummingbird dipped down to sip out of the feeder Austen had hung. "It's nice back here."

"Would almost be peaceful if not for all the hammering and sawing going on inside," Austen joked as banging and whining filtered out from inside.

"It'll totally be worth it when it's finished." Piper dug into the bag and handed over something brown wrapped in plastic.

Austen took it, her stomach growling. "A brownie?"

"Yep. I meant to make you some homemade ones but I ran out of time and had to squeeze in an extra showing this morning. I promise I'll bring some over soon though."

"It's okay, this is awesome. I so needed a sugar fix." Austen bit into it, savoring the rich, chewy treat, and moaned. "Yum."

Biting into her own, Piper smiled. "Yep, the real deal, made with lots of butter and melted chocolate."

They ate in silence for a minute, and Austen studied the other woman. "You look good. Things going better now?"

Piper sighed and finished her mouthful before answering. "I guess. I finally broke down and had Greg served with a restraining order. So far he's abided by it, hasn't called or showed up or 'accidentally' run into me in town. I hated doing it, but he didn't leave me with many other options."

"I'm sorry. But I'm glad you took steps to protect yourself." Hard to understand how Piper had gotten mixed up with someone like Greg. She was so damn nice.

"He didn't always used to be like this," she said softly. "Whatever happened to him on his last tour changed him forever. He came home a completely different person, with a short fuse and no patience for anything. He got help for a while but then he just started drinking to numb everything. Eventually he lost his job as sheriff and that's when he started using drugs. Abusing prescription meds at first, then harder stuff. I tried to help him, but…"

Austen reached over and wrapped her fingers around Piper's hand. "Addiction sucks. And no one can help him except himself."

"I know that. It's why I finally got up the nerve to leave and file for separation. I woke up and realized things were only going to get worse. Part of me feels guilty, like I've abandoned him or something, but I refused to let him drag me down into the muck with him again." She pushed her long bangs out of her face. "It was so damn embarrassing, being tied to him when he'd show up drunk somewhere, or high, or get charged with a DUI. People lost respect not only for him, but for me, too. That was almost as hard as watching him self-destruct right in front of me and not being able to stop it."

Austen squeezed her hand then sat back. "Sorry. I'm glad you got out."

"Me too. It's just been hard to reinvent myself. His family is powerful and wealthy, they have a lot of clout in this state. I'd given up my teaching career to help out with all the charities they ran, always going to functions and fundraisers. It was exhausting, and now I can admit that I didn't love it. I got my real estate license just before we split, so I would have something to help shore up my finances and pay down the debt he put us into."

"Are you gonna go back to teaching?"

"Yep. For now though, real estate sales have been steady and the money's good. I'm paying off the debt slowly but surely and should be in the black by next year if all goes well. I make way more selling real estate than I would from a teacher's salary, so for right now it's working for me. But I've got big plans in the works. It's time to shake things up and start over." Piper waved a hand. "Anyway, enough about me." She leaned forward, her eyes intent on Austen's face. "Tell me about you and Wyatt."

Austen laughed softly. "Wow, don't beat around the bush, okay?"

Piper grinned. "Okay, I won't. So? What's the scoop?" She took a big bite of brownie, her hazel eyes wide and full of interest.

"The honest answer is, I don't really know."

Piper stopped chewing. "What do you mean, you don't know?" she said around the mouthful of brownie, her expression disappointed.

"I don't know where we're at exactly. I think maybe we're seeing each other."

"You *think*?"

"He did just invite me over to dinner at his dad's place, though. He said Easton and their sister might be there."

"Oh, wow." Piper lowered the brownie. "That's huge."

"It is?"

She gave a solemn nod. "Big time. He never asks people over for family dinners. I mean, I don't count, because I'm kind of an honorary Colebrook, but you? Oh yeah." A huge smile spread across her face. "This is so exciting."

Piper's enthusiasm was infectious, but Austen refused to get all worked up over something she wasn't even sure meant anything. "It's not...weird for you? I mean, given that you guys used to date and everything."

Piper made a scoffing sound and waved the concern away. "Not even a little. He barely got to second base and it was a million years ago. Nothing going on with us since we were eighteen, trust me."

Austen almost choked on her brownie at the second base comment.

Piper chuckled. "Did I overshare?"

"I think maybe a little."

"Sorry." She didn't look the least bit apologetic. "It really is ancient history. I'm just thrilled that he's so into you."

"Well then I'm glad." She was pretty thrilled herself.

"He hasn't dated anyone since being wounded, as far as I know. It's been hard to see him shut himself off from everything, but I have a feeling you might be the one to drag him back into the world."

"Yeah?"

"Absolutely. And it couldn't happen to a better guy. It's why I brought Grits to him—I knew for a fact he had to be lonely, and as much as he insisted he didn't want another dog, I knew he'd get attached to the little guy in five minutes flat."

"Wyatt sure does seem to like him."

Piper shrugged. "He just won't admit it out loud, because of masculine pride. He's as alpha as they come, all the Colebrook men are. It's a miracle Charlie managed to date anyone with three older brothers and a former gunnery sergeant dad guarding her."

"I hope I get to meet her tonight. I bet she's got some interesting stories to tell."

"She totally does." Piper slanted her a sly grin. "And I've got a few myself that you might be interested in hearing. If you stick around, that is."

Austen gestured to the gutted house behind her. "Well I'm not planning on leaving anytime soon."

"Good, because Wyatt needs a keeper. You interested?" She stuffed the last of the brownie in her mouth.

Yeah, Austen thought to her surprise. She actually was.

****

He finally knew what he had to do.

The woman was the answer to everything. Austen Sloan.

At first he hadn't been sure, but after seeing her and Wyatt making out in front of the motel last night and then overhearing him invite her to dinner tonight…

Piper had just left the Miller place, and so had the last of the crew. She'd been out back with Austen, neither one of them had noticed him eavesdropping on their highly informative conversation.

Now that he knew, all he had to do was exploit Wyatt's weakness.

The gun in the glove compartment called to him. It would be so easy to go back to the house and take her now. There was no one around to stop him, and he'd catch her off guard. She'd be too surprised, too shocked to do anything but go with him when he held her at gunpoint.

From there he could take her to his hunting shed out in the woods. Tie her down. Maybe have a little fun with her first. She was hot, and the way she'd been so cold and haughty to him made him want to teach her a lesson too.

As soon as the thought formed, he dismissed it. Shaking his head, he blew out an unsteady breath and fought to calm his racing heart.

He couldn't afford to act rashly. He'd never raped a woman before. Never had the urge before. He had to think this through, come up with a solid plan and make his move at just the right time. So he'd go home for the time being and cool off, come up with a solid strategy. After that, all he had to do was shadow her, and sooner or later the right opportunity would appear.

He aimed the dash vent to blow the AC at his face, but even the blast of cold air didn't help clear his head. His damn hands were shaking and he felt queasy.

Christ, he needed a fix, and he needed it now. Even a small one. Anything to dull the pain. For the past three days he'd gone without and he was feeling more unstable than ever. The memories were trapped in his mind, the voices, and the only way to silence them was to get drunk or high. Or both.

His fingers tightened around the steering wheel and he gritted his teeth. Wyatt deserved to be punished for what he'd done. He deserved to suffer.

So he would take Austen from him. Show him what it felt like to lose everything. And part of him dearly wanted Wyatt to see him take her. Wanted to shoot Wyatt first then make him watch, bleeding, while Austen died right in front of him.

He'd take Austen's life while Wyatt was forced to watch, without being able to do a damn thing to save her.

Chapter TWELVE

"Wow, you guys've sure got your work cut out for you with this place," Easton said as he glanced around the front parlor, hands on hips.

"It'll keep us busy for a few months at least, that's for sure," Wyatt answered, reaching out to grasp his father's elbow so he didn't lose his balance and stumble over the materials strewn around the room.

His dad aimed an annoyed glare at him and pulled his arm free. His pride was going to get him seriously hurt one of these days, Wyatt just knew it. "I'm good," he grumbled. "Where's Austen at?"

It surprised him that his dad seemed so eager to see her. She must have made quite an impression on him during last night's dinner. "In the kitchen. Come on back." Both he and Easton had spent time in the Miller house too, before Taylor died, and...on the day of his funeral.

The steady beat of pop music blared from the kitchen, along with the whine of a sander. His dad frowned and shuffled his way toward the sound. "For such a nice girl, she's got shitty taste in music."

Wyatt smirked. "I can't argue with that."

She'd been a good sport by letting him and the other guys listen to their country music for most of the workday during the job. But once the others cleared out for the night, she switched on her stuff and Wyatt tolerated it as best he could.

They rounded the corner of the wall separating the kitchen from the hallway, and Austen was there, her back to them as she sanded down the cabinet doors she'd been working on. Heading for the stereo, Wyatt killed the music.

She straightened and whipped around with an annoyed frown. "Hey, it's my turn—oh!" Breaking into a big smile when she saw his dad and Easton, she pushed the goggles up onto the top of her head. "Came to check the place out, huh? Guess curiosity finally got the better of you."

"All that talk about what you planned for the house last night made me want to see it firsthand," his father said, the left half of his mouth pulled up in a grin. He made his way over to inspect her work, running his left hand over the surface of the cabinet door she'd been working on. "Cherry?"

"Yes. I was going to go with cream or white cabinets because I've always loved a white kitchen, but then I decided it would be better to match the floors. I'm going to stain the cabinets a shade or two darker, then paint the walls a vanilla ice-cream color to make it all pop, and the countertops will be a creamy quartz. With all the light that comes in from the windows, it'll be nice and bright in here even with darker cabinets."

His father nodded in approval as he took in the rest of her work so far. "Looks like you're making good headway." He shook his head, a wry twist to his mouth. "I'm impressed. And I don't impress easy."

"He really doesn't," Easton chimed in.

"You did all this by yourself?" their dad asked her.

"Yep. I love carpentry. There's something special about creating something with my own hands that will be used by someone else for years to come."

"How did you learn it?"

"My grandfather—my mom's dad. My father left us when I was little and my grandpa stepped in to fill that gap. I used to hang out in his workshop with him on the weekends and he started showing me how to do things." She smiled. "My favorite memories of him are the times we spent together working on projects out in his shop behind the house."

"True craftsmanship like this is a dying art form," his father said with an approving nod at her work. Wyatt hid a smile. His dad's opinion of her meant a lot to Wyatt, and it appeared she had him securely wrapped around her finger. She was polite, down to earth and a hard worker, all the things his dad valued most aside from loyalty.

From what Wyatt had seen, she had that too. She was still close to her mom, and her friends back in Pennsylvania. It couldn't have been easy to pick up and move down here after everything she'd been through.

Wyatt admired her courage, her dedication and her work ethic. She worked just as hard as the guys, and most days stayed a couple hours after quitting time to finish something up or tidy up the site. She was also easy to work with and for, huge pluses for him, because he knew how rare that was.

He stayed off to the side while she conversed with his dad and Easton, her easy grin and relaxed manner around his family stealing another piece of his heart. If this kept up, pretty soon she was going to own it completely. He wasn't sure what the exact status of their relationship was, or if they even had one, but that's what he wanted with her.

It would mean having to move outside his comfort zone. Since being wounded he'd become such a recluse and pushed everyone but his family out of his life. Now he wanted to let Austen in. In some ways that was even more terrifying than when he'd finally made the decision to have his lower leg amputated.

Austen cocked her head at his father. "Want to see upstairs? I'll show you how the master suite is coming along."

His dad raised both eyebrows. "Of course I want to see the upstairs."

"Great." Hooking her arm through his in a sneaky but endearing ploy to keep him steady on his feet, she began leading him toward the bottom of the stairs and Wyatt fell for her a little more. His father shot him a smirk but didn't say anything as he followed.

Oh yeah, she definitely had his dad's number. He grinned to himself and turned to Easton, who hadn't moved. "You're not going upstairs?"

"Nah." He tucked his hands into his front pockets and rocked back on his heels. "I barely recognize that look on your face, but it's damn good to see it again."

Wyatt frowned. "What look?"

"You know what I mean." He angled his head toward the stairs, where Austen had just disappeared with their dad. "Her. She makes you happy."

Yeah, she really did.

"I like her," his brother went on. "Piper adores her, and I'm pretty sure dad is smitten. You gonna ask her out officially?"

Wyatt put his hands on his hips. "I might."

"Good." Easton stepped forward to grasp Wyatt's shoulder and squeezed. "Try not to be a miserable son of a bitch, and you be good to her. She's had it rough."

He frowned. "Who told you that?"

"Does it matter?"

"Piper."

Easton didn't deny it. He released Wyatt's shoulder and grinned. "Austen's awesome. I'm happy for you, man."

Wyatt rubbed the back of his neck, feeling awkward. "She's not mine."

"Well then hurry the fuck up and do something about it, dumbass."

Wyatt's gaze strayed back up the stairs as he considered his brother's words. He'd felt half-dead inside for so long and it was like Austen had revived him again.

Pursuing her was a risk, but he'd been living a half-life since being wounded. He of all people knew how short life was, and it was time to start living again to the fullest. Not only for himself, but to honor the guys he'd lost, who had paid the ultimate sacrifice that day.

A few minutes later Austen's voice reached him as she escorted his dad back down the stairs. She tossed him a smile when she came into view, her arm still hooked securely through his father's. "Your dad's pretty damn nimble for someone who suffered a stroke."

"It's all a matter of attitude," his father proclaimed as they neared the bottom step. "Mind over matter. Be damned if I was gonna lay down and die just because of some clot in my brain, or wind up in a wheelchair from it. No sir. Not this Marine."

Wyatt exchanged a conspiratorial grin with Austen that warmed him right to the center of his heart. He wanted time alone with her. So when his dad and brother finally left fifteen minutes later, he didn't wait. "Come over for dinner tonight? My place. Just the two of us."

"And Grits."

"And Grits," he conceded, pulse beating faster because he was pretty sure she was going to say yes.

"I'd love that," she murmured, and leaned in to kiss him. It was way too brief, over before he'd even gotten a taste of her and she pulled back, her silver eyes molten with desire he desperately wanted to quench. "I'll make out with you later, once I'm all freshened up and not all sweaty and covered in sawdust."

"I don't care about any of that," he said, taking her by the shoulders. He didn't give a shit if she was sweaty. He'd happily make out with her right here and now until her knees gave out, then lay her out on the floor, strip her naked and bury his face between her long, strong thighs. God, just the thought of it made blood rush to his groin.

"Well I do." She brushed her lips over the corner of his mouth and straightened. "I'll bring dinner. I'm gonna make you my mama's famous mac 'n cheese. One bite and you'll think you've died and gone to heaven."

He cupped her jaw in one hand, dropped his voice to a deep murmur as he stared into her gorgeous eyes. "I already think that, every time I kiss you."

Her pupils dilated, expanding until only a thin rim of silver showed around the edges. "You keep sweet talking me like that, and you might get more than strawberry shortcake for dessert."

He almost growled, had to order his hand to drop when she stepped back.

"I've just got a couple more things to finish up here. I'll grab the groceries on my way to the motel, clean up and then come right over."

He was already starving, and for way more than her mama's mac 'n cheese. "Looking forward to it."

The smile she tossed him was so sensual and full of promise he went rock hard in his jeans. "Me too. Be safe."

The reminder of the stalker sobered him immediately. "You too," he said as she walked out of the room.

****

Austen got to Wyatt's place at a little before seven that night. She pulled the groceries out of the passenger seat and walked up to the front door of the cabin with anticipation curling in her stomach. For the last few hours all she'd thought about was Wyatt and what it would be like to feel his naked body on top of her. Inside her.

Grits was there at the door to greet her, and Wyatt a second later. He swung open the screen door with one muscular arm and gave her a smile that almost melted her panties. "Hi. You look amazing," he said, taking the bags from her with one hand.

"Thanks." She'd bought this dress at a boutique last summer and never had an occasion to wear it. The bright coral dress was sleeveless and came to mid-thigh, showing off her arms and legs, and the heels she'd put on accentuated the muscles she worked hard to keep in shape. She wasn't a girly girl, but she'd wanted to look her best for him. "You shaved." He looked so different without his dark beard. The swirls and pockmarks on the right side of his face made her want to kiss each one of them. She realized how huge it was, that he was letting her see the full extent of the scars. It touched her deeply.

He rubbed a hand over his clean-shaven jaw. "Yeah. Thought I'd better clean up for you."

"Well, for the record I think your beard is sexy too, but damn, you sure clean up nice."

He smiled and flushed a bit, which she found freaking adorable. "Come on in."

"Thanks." She stepped inside and waited while he placed the groceries on the counter.

"This is a lot of food for just us," he said, glancing in the bags.

"Well, mama's mac 'n cheese recipe makes a whole big casserole dish full so you'll have leftovers tomorrow."

"How many kinds of cheese did you buy?" he asked, sounding astonished as he began unloading everything onto the counter.

"Four. And heavy cream, then butter and breadcrumbs for the top. Not to mention the fixings for dessert later."

At the word dessert he stopped what he was doing and met her gaze, a hungry expression on his face that made her want to skip dinner altogether. She'd worn her hair down tonight, taking extra care to tame her curls into individual spirals that bounced against the tops of her shoulders, and she'd added just enough makeup to accentuate her eyes. Judging by the heated look in Wyatt's eyes as he raked his gaze over her, it had totally been worth the extra effort.

"We could start with dessert," he said in that low, sexy voice that did things to her.

"We could," she allowed, "but I'd hate for you to miss out on the mac 'n cheese." Besides, she was enjoying this slow build way too much to rush now. She wanted to savor this, the entire experience of tonight.

He opened the fridge. "Want some wine? There's still some left from the other night."

"Love some. Can I just make myself at home in here and go for it?"

"Be my guest," he said with a smile, reaching up into a cabinet for a wineglass.

She found a couple of pots, utensils and a cutting board, then got busy grating all the cheeses while the water for the macaroni heated.

Wyatt placed the wine within reach. "Need a hand?"

"No, you just relax," she said while the butter melted in the saucepan. She added the flour and whisked it together to make the roux, then stirred it until it cooked through before adding the milk and heavy cream.

She was adding the first grated cheese when Wyatt stepped up behind her, close enough that she could feel the heat of him through her dress, and settled his big hands on her hips. He nuzzled the back of her neck, and her knees went weak.

"Looks amazing already," he murmured, his lips brushing over her nape. He trailed kisses to the left side of it, to the sensitive spot that made her gasp and lift up on tiptoe.

It took her a moment to realize she was still holding a handful of shredded Gruyere. "You're distracting me."

"Am I?" His teeth raked ever-so-lightly against her skin, then the warm flick of his tongue caressed her.

Her fingers bunched around the cheese as her eyes closed. "At this rate I'm gonna burn your kitchen down."

He chuckled, the warm gust of his breath on her skin sending an arrow of desire through her. "Can't have that, you being a firefighter and all." Placing one more seductive kiss on that spot that made her see stars, he straightened and slipped his arms around her waist, pressing the front of him flush along her back and hips.

"So not helping," she said, her voice all breathy and weak. She'd sensed this in him, the latent sensuality he was showing her now, but she hadn't anticipated how much it would affect her.

"Sorry." His tone made it clear that he wasn't, and he didn't budge, apparently content to tease her with the feel of his strength and the hardness of his erection pressed against her ass. "Maybe I'm taking pointers. I've never made mac 'n cheese before, except from a box."

"That's disgusting and wrong," she said, and finally got control back over her body long enough to add the last of the cheese into the simmering sauce. "Once you try this, you'll never go back."

"Hmm, can't wait to taste it," he murmured, and the sexual tone made her clench her upper thighs together, which only increased the throb between them.

I can't wait either. God, she couldn't ever remember getting this hot and bothered from some flirting. She couldn't even call those little kisses he'd just given her foreplay, because they'd been over too quick. Anxiety danced in her belly when she thought of where things were heading between them tonight. She hadn't been with anyone since John died and the thought of sleeping with Wyatt was both thrilling and a little terrifying. She didn't do flings, hadn't been interested in anyone else until now, and she was nervous.

Finally, he released her and went to feed Grits, enabling her to think again. Once she'd drained and rinsed the partially cooked pasta, she added it to the sauce, stirred it all together and sprinkled buttered breadcrumbs over the top. After tidying up a bit she threw together a quick salad, sliced some fresh, local strawberries and tossed them with sugar while the dish baked in the oven.

Checking the mac 'n cheese, her stomach growled in anticipation when she saw that it was bubbling and the breadcrumbs were a golden brown. "It's ready."

Wyatt had the plates and utensils out by the time she'd pulled it from the oven. "Oh, man, that smells awesome," he groaned.

"Oh, it's better than awesome," she said with pride. "My mom took this to every church potluck we ever went to and people always go crazy for it. She gets requests for it all the time." She glanced over at him. "Where do you want to eat?"

"How about out on the back porch?"

"That sounds perfect." She carried the salad out while he took the hot casserole dish and their plates. Grits trotted outside with them. "Oh, it's a screen porch!" she said, glancing around the cozy space.

A porch swing covered in a long cushion and throw pillows rocked in the breeze at one end, a table and chairs with ottomans sitting opposite it. "My grandmother had one of these at her old place down in Mississippi. I used to sleep out there on a day bed she always made up for me with a pretty quilt on top. It was too hot to sleep with the quilt on, but every morning I put it back on the bed and smoothed it out."

"I love it out here," he answered, setting the mac 'n cheese on a hunting magazine to protect the wooden table. "I've been known to sleep on this swing. I built it extra long and deep to fit me."

The words long and deep made her think of the exact opposite of sleeping. "You built it?"

He flashed her an amused smile. "You're not the only one handy with a saw and hammer."

She sank onto one end of the swing and waited while Wyatt filled a plate for her, motioning with one hand to ask for more mac 'n cheese when he put one measly scoop next to the heap of greens. He sat next to her and she watched as he took his first bite.

He stopped chewing, looked over at her and groaned deep in his chest.

"Good, right?" she asked, that deep rumble of pleasure doing nothing to cool the arousal building inside her.

"Oh, man," he moaned, and immediately scooped up another bite.

"It's the smoked cheddar, I think. The combination of cheese is to die for. Now aren't you glad I made enough for leftovers tomorrow?"

He made a sound of agreement and kept eating. It felt intimate, sitting out here alone with him in this most private spot. Wyatt didn't let many people in, and she was honored that he trusted her enough. "So I've been dying to ask you."

"Ask me what?"

"About that 'family situation' you mentioned at the restaurant the other night."

"Oh." He lowered his plate. "My brother, Brody. He's two years younger than me." Wyatt shook his head, his expression rueful. "It's a hell of a story."

She turned more toward him, curiosity piqued. "Well now I need to hear it."

"I can't tell you everything, but I can give you the basics." He explained about how Brody had met a woman named Trinity, and the danger that had followed, ending up with them in a gunfight in the middle of a cornfield the night Austen had closed the deal on the house.

By the time he finished the story, her eyes were wide. "Holy...cow," she breathed.

"Yeah," he said. "It was intense."

No kidding. "And are they still together?"

He nodded. "She's gone back to London now, but he's crazy about her and wants to make a long distance relationship with her work, even though I know he wants her to move back here with him." He shook his head once, almost in wonder. "I've never seen Brody react like that to a woman before."

Austen smiled at the bewilderment in his tone. "Love makes people do crazy things."

"I guess it does."

She frowned. "What, you've never been in love before?"

"No," he said, lowering his gaze to his plate as he resumed eating, making it clear the change in topic made him uncomfortable.

Really? She found that interesting because she knew he cared about her. From what Piper had said, him inviting her to dinner with his family was a big deal. He'd certainly worked his way into her heart over the past week. She hoped things kept progressing between them, but wasn't going to push, and let it go for now.

After he had seconds, he insisted on cleaning up while she finished making dessert, making the Chantilly whipped cream and spooning it over top of the macerated berries set on top of sponge cakes. He refilled her wine glass and they headed back to the porch swing.

Austen set her empty plate onto the table in front of them and closed her eyes, breathing in the serenity of the moment. The fresh scent of cut grass and the sound of crickets singing drifted on the breeze. "It's so peaceful back here."

"Mmhmm," he agreed around a mouthful of shortcake.

She opened her eyes to take in more of the view. "You said this place has been in your family for generations?"

"Yeah, but this is only what's left of the original homestead. Used to be a lot bigger. My ancestors fought the Yankees in these very fields." He indicated the pasture in front of them with a nod.

She made a disparaging sound. "Damn Yankees."

He grinned. "Yeah. But I like some Yankees just fine." His eyes were warm as he nudged her shoulder.

Her lips twitched. "That's good to hear."

She closed her eyes once more, then opened them and looked down when a shockingly loud snore sounded from the floor. Grits was stretched out on his side at their feet, paws twitching, tail thumping on the floor even in his sleep. "Wow, he's loud."

Wyatt grunted. "You have no idea," he muttered, and swallowed his mouthful. "You should hear him at night. It's like having a friggin' chainsaw at the foot of my bed."

She lifted an eyebrow. "You let him sleep on your bed, huh?"

He hid a smile. "Only for a little while. He gets too hot and jumps down onto the floor. He's like Velcro, I swear. I can't even go to the bathroom alone."

It was clear Wyatt loved the little guy. She adored that such a big, gruff man had so much softness inside him, even if he didn't want to admit it. "You going to keep him?"

He sighed. "Yeah. I can't give him up now. Piper was betting on that, no doubt."

She already loved Piper. "No doubt. I had a long chat with her yesterday."

He met her eyes. "Oh?"

She nodded. "About you. Said you needed a keeper."

He snorted. "Sounds like something she'd say."

Austen grinned. "I dunno, from what I've seen, I think you take pretty good care of yourself. But it's nice to have someone to come over and make you homemade mac 'n cheese then sit out on the back porch with you, right?"

"Yeah. Real nice." He reached one hand up to trail his fingertips down the side of her cheek, then lifted his arm in invitation.

She scooted closer, settling into his side as he curled his strong arm around her shoulders. With a long sigh she rested her head on his sturdy shoulder. It was so nice to relax out here with him, no talking, just enjoying each other's presence.

Her stomach was full, the wine had relaxed her and Wyatt was warm and solid next to her. A languid arousal stole through her, like sun-warmed honey sliding through her veins.

She hadn't known him long. Incredible as it seemed, she was already falling for him, and tonight was going to change things between them forever. She was more than ready to take that next step with him.

So when he cupped her jaw and turned her face toward his, it was the most natural thing in the world to lean into him and press her lips to his.

Chapter THIRTEEN

Wyatt held back a groan of raw need when Austen's lips parted beneath his, inviting him to taste her.

He'd been biding his time throughout dinner and dessert, letting the arousal between them simmer, giving her a chance to change her mind if she had second thoughts about this. Given the way she all but melted against him, her tongue gliding sensually along his, she was totally on board with it.

Sinking his left hand into her hair, he slid his right hand between her shoulder blades to bring her closer. She tasted sweet, like the strawberries they'd just eaten, and she felt so damn good, firm yet soft in all the right places. He wanted all of her, to imprint himself on her so she'd feel him all day tomorrow.

Austen murmured in pleasure and linked her hands around the back of his neck, coming up on her knees to press her breasts to his chest. She ran her hands over his shoulders, down his chest and around to stroke his back.

He was already rock hard in his jeans, the throb getting worse with each slick stroke of her tongue against his.

He let his hands wander, exploring the bare skin of her upper back revealed by the dress, down her ribs to the taut curve of her waist and back up to cup her breasts. They fit in his hands perfectly, the firm curves nestling into his palms.

With an approving sound she sucked at his tongue, gently, slowly, making him crazy to feel that mouth elsewhere. He wanted her hands on him, her luscious mouth teasing and tasting. He wanted to make her addicted to him.

The porch swing creaked as he looped an arm around her waist and hauled her up to straddle his lap. The skirt of her dress fell around her splayed thighs as his mouth found that sensitive spot at the side of her neck.

She gasped and arched, flattening her breasts to his chest, then rubbed her center against the length of his straining, confined cock. It felt so good that he shuddered, his hands locking around her hips, teeth raking over her pulse point. Damn, it had been so long for him, and he'd never felt this way before. He was so comfortable with her, he trusted her, and he cared about her. About her pleasure and protection. He wanted to make her *his*.

"Oh," she whispered, one hand gripping the back of his head, the other holding his palm to her breast.

He wanted her naked, now. He wasn't going to strip her out here in case someone decided to walk the back fields tonight. This was their first time and he wanted her as comfortable as possible. He didn't want anyone to see her but him. She was his, and his possessive streak was off the charts with her.

Part of him was still stunned that Austen wanted him, but he wasn't going to stop this. He couldn't.

Somehow, against all odds, she'd wormed her way into his heart, and he'd damn well be worthy of her, be the kind of man she'd be proud to have at her side.

"Come here," he murmured against her ear, nipping the lobe lightly as he dragged her hips tighter to his. God dammit, the feel of her was driving him nuts. "Wrap your legs around me and hold on."

She shifted up and slipped her legs around his waist, moaning when the friction rubbed his aching dick against the flesh between her thighs. The hand on the back of his head stayed put, her other creeping up to loop around his neck.

Holding her securely around the hips and waist, Wyatt pushed to his feet, pausing a moment to make sure he had his balance. Austen layered frantic kisses across his face, his jaw, teasing his mouth as he walked them to the door leading into the house.

Turning slightly, he shoved it open with one shoulder and carried her through to his bedroom, keeping pressure on her hips to ensure maximum friction along her center as he walked.

Then she locked her ankles behind him and did a swiveling motion with her hips that made him freeze and suck in a breath. It felt like every drop of blood in his body suddenly surged to his groin, and his bedroom suddenly seemed a mile away instead of mere yards.

The couch was way closer than his bed and it was deep enough to hold them both comfortably.

He snagged a blanket from the table behind it to protect her bare skin from sticking to the leather. He shook it out with one hand, then carefully sank to his knees in front of the couch, lowering her onto the center cushion. Immediately she let go of him and reached back to grasp the zipper at the back of her neck.

Wyatt caught her hands in his and brushed his mouth across hers. "Let me do it." He'd fantasized about this for the past ten days, the chance to unwrap her like the best Christmas present in the world.

She gave a little hum of assent and went back to kissing him, her hands on either side of his face. It was damn hard to concentrate on what he was doing but he managed to find the zipper and draw it all the way down, pulling back to inspect what the dress revealed as he lowered the front of it over both firm shoulders and down her chest.

For a moment he could only stare, his heart thumping as the soft material fell away, exposing a white lace bra. Her light brown nipples peeked out at him, hard as they pressed against the lace.

Pushing the dress to her waist, he let his fingers trail reverently over the upper curves, delighting in the goose bumps that formed beneath his touch. Her breathing came faster now, her body still except for the way her breasts rose and fell with each excited breath.

Dying to put his mouth to her, he pulled the lace cups down and left the bra in place, the bunched-up material pushing the mounds higher. Her nipples beaded tighter, and he couldn't wait a moment longer.

An instant before his tongue touched the first one, something licked his forearm. Jerking his head back, he blinked down at Grits, who had his front paws on the couch, tongue hanging out as he panted and wagged his tail.

Cock blocked by a twenty-pound lapdog, he thought in rueful dismay. Cavaliers were known as the love sponges of the dog world, but this was ridiculous.

Austen giggled. Suppressing his irritation, Wyatt snapped his fingers and pointed to the corner of the room. "Grits. Bed."

The dog froze then lowered his head in submission.

"*Bed*," he commanded, pointing again. "Now."

Dropping his front paws to the floor, Grits slunk away to his bed in the corner and lay down, clearly not happy about it but obeying nonetheless.

"Stay," Wyatt ordered. When he was sure the dog would obey, he turned back to Austen with an apologetic grin. "Sorry. Where was I?"

"Right here," she murmured, her voice husky with arousal and need he was dying to satisfy as she drew his head back to her breast and arched her spine.

Wyatt couldn't hold back a groan as he gripped her ribcage and licked at the taut nipple. Austen hissed in a breath and dug her fingers into his head, pushing her breast harder into his mouth.

He laved the tender flesh a few times then gave into the need burning inside him and drew it into his mouth. Her soft whimper of pleasure made the ache between his legs worthwhile.

She squirmed beneath him, reached for his shoulders and began drawing up his shirt. Wyatt released her nipple long enough to peel the shirt over his head and toss it aside, pleasure racing through him when her hands began roaming over his bare chest and back.

Cupping her breasts in his hands he worked his way south, kissing and nipping at the smooth skin of her stomach, her abdomen. He reached the white lace panel on the front of her panties and pressed his mouth there, inhaling the heady scent of her arousal.

"God, Wyatt…"

He pulled her panties down, stilled for a moment and swallowed a ragged groan when he saw that she was completely bare between her legs. *Oh, sweet Jesus.*

Dropping her panties on the floor, he put a hand on the inside of either thigh and stroked his fingertips gently up and down the center of her mound. She whimpered at the delicate touch and raised her hips, and he couldn't take any more.

Lowering his head, he pressed his mouth to those delicate folds, let his tongue sweep over them, up to graze the taut nub of her clit. Austen sucked in a breath and grabbed his head, her long legs wrapping around his shoulders.

Oh yeah, baby, get comfortable. He planned on doing this for a good long while.

His cock was so swollen it hurt as he licked and sucked at her softest flesh, quickly learning what pressure she liked. He gave her exactly what she asked for, following the cues of her whimpers and sighs, the pressure of her hands on the back of his head. Then he pushed his tongue into her and she cried out his name, her body arching like a drawn bow.

"Get inside me," she panted, legs quivering.

Wyatt dug his wallet out of his jeans pocket and pulled out a condom before shucking his shoes, pants and underwear. He knew how fast gossip spread in this town so rather than hit the drugstore for protection this afternoon, he'd driven to the next town over to buy condoms.

Balanced on one knee he reached for her, turning her so that she lay lengthwise on the couch. Austen dragged him forward, her strength surprising him for a moment before her hand curled around his cock. His head dropped forward on a rough groan as she pumped him in a firm grip that damn near made his eyes roll into the back of his head.

After a few strokes he grabbed her hand to stop her, rolled the condom on and settled between her thighs. She wrapped her legs around his hips and pulled him close, undulating beneath him in a sensuous wave, her eyes heavy-lidded with desire.

Through the haze of lust and desire he had a fleeting moment of self-consciousness that he still had his prosthetic on. She couldn't see it though, and for damn sure it wouldn't affect his performance, so he pushed it out of his mind and came down to brace his elbows on either side of her head.

The way her eyes smoldered up at him set his heart racing. God, it had never been like this for him. She made him want to devour her, even as another part of him yearned to cherish her. Holding her gaze, he reached down to align himself and pushed forward. Snug, slick heat enveloped him.

He moaned and pushed deeper, capturing her soft cry with his mouth, his tongue sliding into her as his cock sank deep. They both shuddered, Austen gripping his shoulders tight.

Sweat broke out across his back. He caressed her tongue with his, stroked the roof of her mouth as he eased his hips back and thrust forward once more. The friction felt unbelievable, every nerve ending sizzling at the contact. He built a slow rhythm, then shifted higher onto his knees to reach one hand down between them and rub her swollen clit.

"Yes, like that," she gasped out and rocked upward, grinding her pelvis against his.

Wyatt gritted his teeth as the pressure and heat built, her sighs and whimpers driving him higher and higher. Just when he was about to pull out to keep from exploding too soon, her inner walls clenched around him and she threw her head back, crying out as she began to come.

So damn beautiful. He rode out the pulses of her release while staring down into her face, and the expression of ecstasy written there undid him.

Pressing his face into her neck, he gripped handfuls of her curls and thrust deep, shouting as his own release hit. Pleasure blasted through him, raw and powerful. It punched through his entire body, making every muscle quake, leaving him spent and shaken. When it faded he collapsed on top of her with a low groan, panting, heart thundering in his chest.

Austen made a murmuring sound and ran a hand through his hair, skimmed it down his neck, over his damp shoulders and back. Her touch was damn near drugging, her strong curves supporting his greater weight.

Summoning his strength after a few minutes he rolled them to reverse their positions, bringing her on top of him. Austen sighed and snuggled into his hold, her cheek nestled on his shoulder, the warm weight of her body draped over his. In the comfortable silence he ran his hands up and down the length of her naked back, over the firm globes of her ass. Christ, he couldn't get over the feel of her, or how well they fit together. Her skin was like warm satin beneath his palms.

Lying here with her in his arms, he couldn't ever remember feeling this content. A sense of masculine pride filled him in knowing that he'd satisfied her. Closing his eyes, he savored the peace inside him. For years he'd shut himself off from others but with Austen his heart was wide open. There were no words needed as he held her, basking in the quiet comfort of her presence.

Until the sound of little paws racing on the plank floor broke through his serenity. Then the racing turned into a hopping.

Austen raised her head from his chest to look for the dog. "What's he doing?"

"Chasing a fly," Wyatt said on a sigh without opening his eyes.

"What? Seriously?" She half pushed up to look and Wyatt cracked his left eye open in time to see Grits hop by on his hind legs, like a furry pogo stick as he tracked the fly across the living room. Austen let out a delighted laugh. "He's so funny."

He grunted and closed his eye. *Yeah. So funny.*

Then she gave a sharp gasp that had his eyes shooting open, and scrambled upright, grabbing her discarded dress from the floor to shield herself. "Wyatt."

He was already sitting up and pushing her behind him, the urgency in her voice sending a chill down his spine as he followed her gaze toward the tall window at the far end of the room. "What?"

"I saw someone at the window. They were wearing a mask." Her voice was edged with fear.

A fierce protectiveness roared through him. "Stay here," he ordered, pushing her off him and dragging his clothes on. As soon as he had his jeans up his legs, he pulled out his phone and called Easton. "Someone's prowling on the property. Austen said she just saw someone in the window, wearing a mask."

"Shit. I'll meet you out back right now, and Dad will stay with Austen."

"Okay."

Wyatt raced to his bedroom to grab a pistol and tactical flashlight from his bedside table, then hurried back to the living room to get his boots on. Whoever the fuck had been playing peeping Tom at his window, they weren't getting far.

Austen was already dressed and without a word quickly knelt to help him tie his other boot. "What are you going to do?" she asked, shooting him an anxious look as she stood.

"Gonna go after whoever that was at the window." God, he hadn't even thought about shutting the blinds, he'd been too wrapped up in her, and had never thought someone would come around here.

"You think it's the same person who sent the texts?" Her tone was tense.

"Don't know, but maybe." He stood, gripped her shoulder and looked into her wide silver eyes. "Stay put, no matter what. My dad will be over to stay with you in a minute, okay? Promise me you'll wait here, and out of sight."

She nodded once. "I promise. But just…be careful, okay?"

He gave a terse nod then kissed her once, hard. She was his and he wasn't taking any chances with her safety.

Easton bounded up the front porch and threw the door open. "Which way?" he asked, a rifle in his hands.

"Out here," Wyatt said, and led the way through to the screen porch and out the door to the backyard.

Immediately he went to the back window and looked at the ground. Several partial footprints indented the earth beside the cabin wall.

Using the high-powered beam of the flashlight, he aimed it at the prints and followed them. They seemed to lead east, toward one of the pastures, and the woods beyond.

"Take Sarge with you," his dad called from inside, pushing open the door to let the basset hound out.

Wyatt didn't have time to wait around, but he gave the dog a terse command. "Sarge. Track," he said, pointing to the prints in the earth.

The basset trotted over and lowered its nose to the ground, started snuffling as Wyatt and Easton followed the direction of the trail of prints. Wyatt took the lead, was halfway to the pasture when he heard Sarge's low *woof* behind him. Two seconds later the dog was passing him, his nose to the ground, tail high.

"He's got the scent," he called back to Easton, a surge of adrenaline rushing through him. This was so familiar, the chase, the hunt. And damned if it didn't feel good to be back in action again.

The sounds and scents of the night filtered out around him as he followed Sarge at a jog, Easton right behind him. He liked knowing his brother was at his back.

Up ahead Sarge paused at the white-painted fence marking the edge of one of the grazing pastures. He sniffed around it, running back and forth.

An uneasy feeling crawled up Wyatt's spine. If the trespasser had a weapon he could easily conceal himself in the brush at the edge of the forest. The bright beam of the flashlight would make Wyatt and Easton instant targets. He wanted to shine it toward the forest in case he caught a glimpse of their trespasser, but held off.

Sarge gave another woof and squeezed under the fence, then took off at an angle across the pasture. Wyatt vaulted the fence, making sure he landed with more pressure on his good leg. Easton was right behind him, and gave chase. At the edge of the forest Sarge paused again and sniffed around, tracking back and forth, back and forth.

Wyatt glanced around, but there wasn't enough light to see anything beyond shadows and branches close to him. "See anything?" he whispered to Easton.

"No."

Sarge moved into the underbrush and through the forest, sniffing here and there. Wyatt followed, and a few minutes later the dog let out a low bark. Wyatt rushed over to where the basset waited near where the forest gave way to the road, saw something on the ground. Lowering himself to one knee, not daring to use the flashlight, he picked up the item on the ground.

A rubber Halloween mask.

Cursing under his breath, he stood and showed it to Easton, then glanced over at Sarge. The basset was sniffing at the shoulder of the road just beyond the trees. He'd clearly lost the scent and was wandering around in a frustrated circle, trying to pick it up again.

Wyatt knew it was a lost cause. Without being able to use the flashlight they were blind out here, and whoever had worn the mask was long gone in whatever vehicle he'd parked here. From this side of the woods he could have taken any one of three separate roads away from here, and without a direction or clue, there was no way to follow. Why had the guy left the mask? Had to have dropped it on the run, by accident.

"Guess that's it," Easton said, his tone full of disappointment.

"Yeah." Wyatt whistled softly to recall Sarge, reached down to stroke the dog's long, velvety ears. "Good boy," he murmured. For such an old hound, he'd done well to track the suspect this far.

"You want to head back and drive around to the road, see if we can find tracks?"

Wyatt shook his head. "It's been so dry here I doubt there'd be any tracks even if he drove here and left his vehicle on the shoulder of the road. I'll call the cops."

Together they headed back to the cabin, while Wyatt called to report it. When they arrived Austen rushed out into the backyard to meet them. Her arms were wrapped around her waist, her expression anxious. He hated seeing her scared. "Anything?"

"Just this." Wyatt held out the mask they'd found.

"Yes, that's what I saw," she confirmed, and when she looked back up at him he could see the fear in her eyes.

"Whoever it was is long gone now," he said, pulling her into his arms. "The cops are gonna take a look around the property line tonight and someone will come out in the morning to gather more evidence." She pressed close as he hugged her tight and kissed the top of her head, her springy curls tickling his nose and lips. "You okay?" he murmured, needing to make her feel safe.

"Yes. You?"

"Yeah, I'm good." He looked over the top of her head at his dad and brother. "Thanks for your help. I'll talk to the cops about it in the morning."

His father shot a glance at Austen, a frown wrinkling his forehead. "Until we know what's going on, maybe it's best she stay here with you. I don't want her being alone in that motel after this."

Wyatt nodded. "I didn't plan on letting her go."

The ghost of a smile teased his father's lips. "Good. Come on, Easton," he said, waving his free hand toward the front door. "Let's get outta here. Come on, Sarge."

Wyatt released Austen long enough to shut and lock the screen porch door behind him, then the door leading to the interior of the house. "Let's pull all the blinds."

She helped him, securing all the windows and doors before meeting him in the kitchen.

"You okay with staying the night?" he asked.

She nodded. "I was hoping to anyway, just under different circumstances."

He brushed a spiral curl away from her cheek. "Then forget what happened. I'm here and I'm not going to let anything happen to you."

A slow smile curved her mouth. "That shouldn't be romantic, but it is."

He held out a hand. "Come to bed."

She slipped her hand into his, the trust and heat in her eyes making his heart turn over. And in that moment, despite the trespasser, he realized that for the first time since he'd been wounded, he was happy, and excited about his life. It was easy to envision a future with her. Crazy as it would have seemed a few weeks ago, he was falling hard and didn't want to ever let her go.

****

Shit, that had been way too close.

His heart pounded like a jackhammer as he drove down the deserted road that took him away from the Colebrook's property, and not simply because he was high.

He'd wanted to spy on Wyatt and Austen, see if there might be an opportunity to take her, maybe when she got into her truck as she left the cabin. But when he'd crept to the back of it and heard what was going on inside, he couldn't resist the opportunity to watch.

Wyatt Colebrook was fucking the boss. And enjoying every moment of it, from what he'd seen tonight.

He'd never thought of himself as a voyeur, but Austen was so fucking hot that for those few minutes he'd stood watching through the window, he'd been so caught up he'd actually been able to get past the fact that she'd been screwing Wyatt.

Instead he'd imagined it was him on top of her, inside her. She'd been breathtaking in her sensuality, head flung back, and those sounds she'd made…God.

His dick throbbed in time with each heartbeat as he thought of her. He hadn't fucked a woman since he'd hooked up with that escort after his bitch of a wife had left him. If a scarred freak like Wyatt could get laid by a woman like Austen, then why shouldn't he?

Maybe when he took her he'd get enough time to enjoy her before Wyatt came after her. Then he'd show her what it felt like to be fucked by a real man, not some footless, scarred cripple.

He swallowed hard as the erotic image of it formed in his mind. Of Austen tied to a bedframe, naked, her beautiful mouth covered in duct tape while he satisfied himself using her body.

Headlights flashed in his rearview mirror as a car turned onto the road a quarter mile behind him. His heart stuttered, then picked up again at double time. But the car didn't race after him, and when he turned east at the next road, it didn't follow.

Letting out a sigh of relief, he headed for home. If Wyatt had called the cops, they wouldn't have much evidence to find him with. He'd lost his mask during the run through the woods but that shouldn't matter.

Even if they found fingerprints or DNA on it they wouldn't find them in time. He'd been careful not to stash his car where it might leave tracks. No one suspected he was up to anything.

Now that he'd seen how involved Wyatt and Austen were, he could pull off the attack any time. He was ready for it. All he needed was the right opportunity. Sooner or later, Wyatt wouldn't be around to protect her.

When that moment came, he would take his revenge.

Chapter FOURTEEN

Austen's eyes flew open in the middle of the night when the mattress bounced. She focused on Wyatt, unsure what had woken her. He was sleeping on his side, turned away from her. He twitched and jerked but didn't wake and his breathing was harsh.

Before she could reach out to touch his shoulder, Grits was standing beside the bed, front paws braced on the edge of it as he licked Wyatt's face.

Wyatt grunted and opened his eyes, half pushing up onto his elbows as he looked wildly around the room. The moonlight filtering through the slats in the blinds showed the sweat glistening on his forehead.

"You okay?" she whispered when he focused on her.

Frowning, he nodded, then pushed at Grits. "Stop. No kisses," he said, his voice rough with sleep, a little out of breath. Then he sat up and turned to swing his legs over the edge of the bed, ran a hand over his face with a hard sigh.

Austen placed a tentative hand on the middle of his broad back and rubbed gently. His muscles twitched beneath her palm but he didn't pull away, so she took that as a good sign. She noticed he was absently petting Grits with one hand as he sat there, getting his breath back.

"Nightmare?" she asked.

He nodded.

She waited a beat, unsure whether to be quiet or try to get him to talk about it. "Do you get them often?"

"Not as often as I used to." He sighed, let his head drop back, one hand still petting Grits.

"He sensed you were in distress even before I did," she told him. "By the time I woke up and realized you were having a bad dream, Grits was already there trying to wake you up."

Wyatt glanced down at the dog. "He's done it a couple times before." He ruffled Grits's ears. "Good boy." Grits cocked his head and wagged his tail harder. Then he whined and Wyatt picked the dog up to set him on his lap. Grits settled against him and started licking. "No kisses," he said in a gruff tone, but there was no heat in it.

Yeah, good luck with that. Grits was determined to love on him.

After a minute Wyatt set him back on the floor. When he didn't say anything else or lie back down, she pushed to her knees and crawled up behind him to press against his bare back, wrapping her arms around his chest. He put one big hand on her forearm and rubbed gently. She laid her cheek against the top of his shoulder and just held him.

After a few minutes he let out a deep breath and relaxed fully. "Sorry about that."

"Nothing to be sorry about." She kissed his shoulder and snuggled up close. "Can I do anything?"

160

"You already did. It doesn't happen that much anymore. Maybe knowing someone was looking in the window earlier triggered it, I don't know."

She made a soft sound to let him know she was listening but didn't interrupt, drawing little patterns on his chest with her fingertips. His chest hair tickled her skin.

"When I was first wounded I had the same dream— or pretty much—every damn night, for months. Now it's down to once every couple weeks or so."

"About Afghanistan?"

Another nod. "That mission. When the firing started, Raider was about a dozen yards away from me. I'd detached her lead and told her to go scout up ahead for our foot patrol. During the ambush I was so busy returning fire, I didn't watch her closely enough. By the time I looked up and saw her sitting to alert me there was an IED there, it was too late. They remote detonated it."

God, how terrifying and awful for him.

"The explosion sent me flying. I didn't even feel the pain at first. The moment I came to I opened my eyes and looked for Raider. I couldn't see much because of all the blood, and I didn't realize yet that I'd lost my right eye. She was lying a few feet away from me, both front legs missing."

Austen closed her eyes and squeezed him tighter.

"I crawled over to her," he said, voice catching. "She was still alive, looking up at me with that glassy-eyed expression I'll never forget. There was nothing I could do for her. By the time the corpsman got to me she was already gone, and so were the guys with me."

He was silent a long moment, and she could feel the tension in his big body. A silent vibration of self-recrimination and grief. "They loaded her onto the Medevac helo with me. One of the guys covered her with an American flag, just like they would any other fallen Marine. Because that's what she was, and that's what pisses me off so much when people say dumb shit like, 'it was only a dog'. Or that the Corps considered her to be a piece of equipment."

He shook his head, the motion full of anger and disgust. "I trained her from the ground up. She trusted me, was the most loyal friend I've ever known, and she saved so many lives over there. Out in the field she slept beside me, or across my legs, and alerted us to any trouble long before we were aware of it. She wasn't just a dog, she was a Marine. My battle buddy. And I let her down."

Tears pricked the back of Austen's eyes. She held him tight, aching for him and all he'd gone through. "Did she know you were there, do you think? At the end?"

"Yeah. Yeah, she knew I was there. That's the only thing I don't regret about that day. I was right there holding her when she died."

While he'd been lying there with a badly lacerated face and a mangled foot and lower leg. God, she hated that he'd gone through all that. "She sounds like a very special Marine."

"She was. At the hospital in Germany, they gave me her purple heart. I put it on her collar. It's on the mantel."

"I saw it." She rubbed her cheek against him. "How long were you in the hospital?"

"Total?"

"Yes."

"Better part of a year, on and off. I had eleven surgeries to try and save my leg before I finally made the call to have it amputated. In hindsight, I wish I'd done it right away. Would've saved me months of recovery."

"Must have been a hard decision."

"Not by that point, not really. It was more of a relief to make the pain stop. I had phantom pain and itching for a while after, but nothing close to what I had before that."

"At dinner the other night I saw a picture of you in the hospital, with your family around you."

"When I was first transferred home. Brody flew in to see me in Germany and stayed for a few days until I was sent back to the States. Easton was deployed overseas and Charlie and my dad were at home. But the day I landed in Virginia, they were all right there for me."

"I think I love your family."

"Yeah, me too." He swiveled his head around toward her. Grasping her hand, he tugged her forward. "Come around here where I can see you."

It was then she realized that she'd been kneeling at his right side, his blind spot. "Sorry."

"It's okay." He drew her around to his left side and brushed the hair back from her face. "Thanks," he said quietly. "Feels good to talk about her with you."

She put a hand on the side of his face, ran her thumb over his cheek. "I'm glad you told me more about her."

Scooting closer, she leaned in to brush her lips across his. His hand delved into her hair, strong fingers cradling the back of her head as he slanted his mouth over hers. She stopped, pulled back. "Where did Grits kiss you?"

Wyatt let out a low laugh. "My cheek and my ear."

"Oh, good." Smiling, she kissed him again. "Don't want my lips where he's already been. Plus, I don't share, I'm greedy like that." The way he held her, and the feel of his lips and tongue against hers had her melting inside.

Unsatisfied to merely lean against him, she swung a leg over his lap and balanced her weight on her knees on the edge of the mattress, straddling him. He gave an approving groan and grasped her hips, fingers squeezing in a dominant grip that fired her arousal even more.

"Grits. Bed," she ordered, pointing at the bed in the corner. She didn't need an audience for this, let alone one so close up. To her surprise the dog got up and padded over to the bed, then flopped down with a dejected sigh.

"Look at you, going all dog whisperer," Wyatt murmured, a smile in his voice.

She hummed against his lips. "I was inspired."

There was so much of him to explore and she hadn't had her fill of him earlier. She ran her hands over his shoulders and chest, down his arms and back up, excited by the feel of those powerful muscles. "You're just so damn sexy, it's hard to stop touching you."

"So then don't," he whispered, nipping at her chin, his deep, intimate tone making heat build between her legs.

Leaning back to watch his face, she skimmed her hands down his chest, his stomach. He got distracted by her breasts, cupping them in his big hands, squeezing gently.

She sighed and let her eyes close for just a moment to enjoy the feel of his thumbs teasing her nipples, then forced her heavy eyelids open and focused on him. He'd been more than generous with her earlier. Right now she wanted to do the same for him. Wipe away the last remnants of the nightmare, replace the painful memories with something good.

Reaching between them, she curled her fingers around the hot, hard length of his erection standing up against his belly. He groaned and pushed into her touch, leaning forward to capture a nipple in his mouth. The feel of his tongue sliding over her sensitive flesh made her moan and squirm, momentarily distracting her from the job at hand.

When he pulled back, releasing her nipple with a quiet pop, she seized her moment and scooted to her knees on the floor in front of him so he wouldn't have to move, her hand still wrapped around his hard length. She looked up at him and gave him a slow, firm stroke, licked her lips so there was no way he could misunderstand what she wanted.

In the faint light coming through the upper windows his eyes gleamed with raw hunger, the sound of his erratic breathing in the silence increasing the erotic tension. The hand in her hair tightened a moment, then relaxed, his fingers rubbing at her curls. An electric silence built between them as she stared up into his eyes and let her free hand caress down the length of his thigh.

His right one, full of scars. Some were deep pits, others raised and bumpy, some smooth, thin lines from a surgeon's scalpel. She ran her hand down to his knee, lower, right over the amputation site, to show him there was no part of him that bothered or disgusted her. That she thought every part of him was beautiful.

And when she bent her head at last and ran her tongue up the length of his cock, he hissed in a breath, his fingers contracting in her hair, the muscles in his chest and arms standing out in sharp relief.

Lowering her gaze, Austen took him between her lips, flicking her tongue against the sensitive underside of the head before sucking. Softly at first, then harder.

Wyatt growled and flexed his hips slightly. "God, sweetheart, that feels so good..."

Hearing that endearment in his low, impassioned voice sent a pleasurable shiver up her spine. She hummed in agreement and took him deeper, built a rhythm with her hand and mouth. He was thick and hot against her tongue, swollen to bursting. It was incredibly arousing to kneel before this strong, sexy man and reduce him to a trembling mass of pleasure with her mouth.

"It's not gonna take me long," he rasped out, gasping as she sucked and let her fingers trail down to caress the soft flesh between his splayed thighs.

She didn't mind, and he was so thick her jaw was already aching. But she didn't let up, following his cues, repeating the motion and pressure he seemed to like best. He was panting now, deep, raw groans coming from the back of his throat.

"I'm gonna come," he warned in a low voice, his big body twitching.

Austen redoubled her efforts, stayed with him until he arched and let go, swallowing his release. After a few moments he sighed and relaxed, began petting her hair. Carefully releasing him, she went into his arms as he pulled her into his lap.

"God, I think you destroyed me," he murmured against her hair, squeezing her tight.

She kissed his neck, his shoulder. "You taste good."

He shuddered at her words, then eased a hand down her side to cup her breast. Her nipple was already beaded tight, and the feel of his thumb and forefinger rolling it lightly made her gasp and bite her lip. More heat rushed through her, settling between her legs where she was slick and ready.

His mouth was at her temple, her ear. "Did sucking me off turn you on, sweetheart? On your knees, taking my cock into that soft little mouth?"

Her eyes nearly crossed at those dirty words spoken in his deep voice. God, just when she thought he couldn't be any sexier.

And he wasn't done. "Is your pussy wet for me, Austen?"

She shivered, could only manage a nod as his mouth found that perfect spot at the juncture of her neck and shoulder and his free hand eased down her middle, his big palm cupping her sex. The warmth of his palm made her whimper, her body hungry for more.

"Mmm, all hot and wet for me," he whispered, his tongue laving her neck while his fingers toyed with her nipple and his other hand stroked between her slick folds.

She trembled in his grasp, reached up to grab hold of his wide shoulders for support and closed her eyes, giving herself over completely to his care.

"Spread your legs for me."

She did as he told her, perched precariously on his lap. But she knew he'd never let her fall.

His fingers caressed each sensitive fold as they stroked up, up to her swollen clit and gently circled it. Her thighs tensed and she moaned, sensation shooting out from her captive nipple and where he was rubbing her so sweetly.

Then he pushed a finger into her and her internal muscles immediately clamped down on it, greedy for more. His mouth trailed hot, wet kisses up her neck to her jaw, his voice and the raw words he used pushing her up the cliff fast.

"So hot, Austen. So fucking sexy. All mine."

She nodded in agreement, gripping his shoulders tighter. She was his, and it floored her. Just weeks ago she'd come here seeking space, a new life. She'd never seen him—this—coming, but she wouldn't change things now.

Over and over he stroked her clit as he thrust his finger into her, rubbing that hidden glow inside her until it felt like she would explode.

"I love stroking your sweet spots," he murmured against her ear. "Almost as much as I loved burying my face in this sweet pussy earlier. Did you like my tongue on your clit? Inside you?"

She shuddered, cried out as she contracted around his finger, the pleasure rising sharp and clear. He didn't stop what he was doing, didn't speed up, seemingly content to drive her out of her mind, her mewls of need mixing with the slick sound of his fingers as they worked her most sensitive flesh.

Then the fingers squeezing her nipple tightened, adding pressure, and the increased sensation set her off. Her wild moan of sweet relief filled the room as the orgasm hit, blinding her with an explosion of pleasure.

Panting as it faded, she collapsed on his chest, her face resting against his neck. Wyatt slid one arm around her and eased his hand from between her legs, pressing tender kisses to her temple and cheek. "I'm glad you were here tonight," he whispered in the quiet.

"Me too." He'd let her in when he felt vulnerable, and hadn't pushed her away. That was huge and their bond was even stronger now.

Nearly boneless with relaxation, she let out a contented sigh when he lay back down and turned them so she was nestled against his side, her head in the crook of his shoulder. She'd never thought she would find someone she'd want to share her life with again, but that's exactly what she'd found in Wyatt.

After pulling the covers over them, he wrapped both arms around her, squeezing tight for a moment as he kissed the top of her head. "Night."

"Night," she whispered back.

Lying safe in his arms with his heart beating beneath her cheek in the moments before she slid into sleep, she smiled to herself. As incredible as it seemed, she'd fallen in love again.

Chapter FIFTEEN

If she was this tired at seven in the morning, it was going to be a long day. Although considering the reason for her tiredness, she had no regrets. After last night's scare, Wyatt had insisted that Easton follow her here and check the place out before she went inside.

Stifling a yawn, Austen smiled as she headed up the front steps of her gutted house, where Easton waited by the front door. "All good," he told her with a smile. "I'll hang out in my truck until the guys get here."

"Thanks, I appreciate it." It made her feel better to know he was looking out for her.

"No problem. Have a good one."

"I will." She headed inside and through to the kitchen, her mind on last night. After Wyatt's nightmare she'd slept tucked against his chest, and woken later to the blissful feel of his hands smoothing over her naked body.

He'd caressed her everywhere, lavishing attention on her most sensitive spots until she was writhing, then turned her onto her stomach and entered her from behind, sliding one hand beneath her to cup her mound and stroke her to orgasm.

After finally crawling out of bed they'd showered together and eaten a quick breakfast out on the screen porch. Right after that he'd left to talk to the police and she'd stopped by the motel to change into her work clothes.

She hadn't been this happy in a long time. It felt foreign, but that only made her appreciate it all the more, because she knew how precious it was. Without a doubt she loved that man, and each day it seemed she drew him more out of his shell. He'd opened up to her so much last night; she hadn't felt this close to anyone other than John.

Although she and Wyatt hadn't known each other long, she refused to obsess over that. They had a fundamental trust between them, a quality she considered to be the most important basis for any relationship.

There were so many things about him that she admired. She loved the way he took care of his family and the people around him, including vets like the guys on the work crew. She loved how he owned up to his responsibilities and stood by his word. She also adored how he treated and touched her.

The inside of the house was quiet and still as she entered the kitchen, the smell of sawdust reminding her of her grandfather. Getting here first at this time of day gave her a lovely respite before the rest of the crew showed up.

Opening the doors that led out to the deck off the kitchen, she stood there a moment, surveying her domain, then let out a contented sigh and closed her eyes. A smile curved her mouth as the early sunrays bathed her face and birdsong filled the air, along with the quiet rustling of leaves in the soft morning breeze.

Once she got the deck refinished and tidied up the landscaping in the yard, it was going to be paradise back here. And she definitely wanted to build a porch swing for back here, because it would remind her of Wyatt. They could have morning coffee out here, or sit together in the evenings and enjoy the tranquility of the private yard.

Back inside she hauled out the finishing supplies she'd bought for the cabinets. Brushes, cloths, stain, varnish. She wanted to get a jumpstart on them before the others arrived so there'd be less dust in the air. She'd already sanded the doors to a satin-fine finish and added the embellishments, so she was anxious to get them stained and done so she could move on to the woodwork on the main staircase.

The sound of footsteps behind made her turn around. Eddie stood framed in the doorway between the kitchen and hall. She straightened, her spine pulling tight as a ribbon of unease coiled in her stomach. "Hey," she said, keeping her expression neutral even though her instinct was to back away.

"Morning. Easton just left." He frowned slightly as his gaze lingered on her face. "You look tired. Long night?"

For just a second his words sent a shiver of alarm through her. Easton was gone. There'd always been something…off about Eddie, something she couldn't quite put her finger on. And he always watched her too intently. He'd suffered a bad head injury and was a bit on the slow side, but… Could he have been the one to send those texts to Wyatt? Had he been at the window wearing that mask last night?

She made sure to keep her face impassive and not betray her suspicion. "No, I'm good. Scott here with you?" Now she wished Easton had stayed. When Wyatt got here she'd pull him aside and ask him to make sure she wasn't left alone on site with Eddie.

"Just pulling up."

"Okay." That made her feel a bit better, and Wyatt would be here as soon as he could. Hopefully with a lead, or some sort of good news about the investigation.

"Where's Wyatt?"

Her gaze moved past Eddie and through the open front door as a car parked out front. Scott. "He'll be here soon."

The lie rolled off her tongue without a second thought. She didn't want him or Scott to know she was alone here with them for long, and refused to feel bad about it, because they didn't need to know why he was down at the police station.

"You gonna start prepping the walls upstairs?" she asked, determined to keep the conversation work-oriented.

"That's the plan."

Her heart beat faster when he kept staring at her, then reached one arm behind him. The trickle of alarm turned into a torrent as he drew something from his back pocket, but it was only a pair of goggles, and she inwardly berated herself for being so paranoid. Last night's situation must have rattled her more than she'd realized. "Scott and me will get started in the master bedroom," he said. "See you in a while."

"Yeah."

When he turned and jogged up the stairs, she blew out a breath and shook her head at herself. Creepy though Eddie might be at times, neither he nor any of the others had been anything but polite to her from day one. Maybe he was harmless. Maybe her gut was wrong.

She took the cabinet doors outside onto the back deck to work on them. In the midst of setting them on the sawhorses, she noticed some staining on a couple of them and bent to take a closer look.

Cursing softly, she ran her fingers over the wood grain marked with some sort of liquid. Maybe one of the guys had spilled something on them yesterday and she hadn't noticed.

Lips pursed, she let out an irritated sigh. The only way to fix it was to sand the entire front down again, and hope to hell she could salvage the doors that way. She'd put too much work into them to have to start over again now.

She wasn't alone with Eddie anymore so she went back inside to get her sander, then put on her tunes. The pop music Wyatt seemed to hate so much flooding out the kitchen doors, as she slipped on her goggles and mask. Turning on the sander, she got busy.

A few moments after she got to work, everything else fell away as it always did when she was working on a project. The beat of the music came through the loud whine of the sander as she moved it over the wood, a fine cloud of sawdust rising into the air.

After a few passes she stopped to check her progress, almost holding her breath. *Please let it work, please let it work...*

Only half of the stain had come off. Her heart sank.

"Dammit," she muttered, scowling as she turned the sander back on. She couldn't take off much more of the wood's surface without damaging all the detail she'd worked so hard on adding.

Carefully moving the sander over the stubborn part of the stain, all her focus was on the task at hand. When noises began penetrating her awareness, at first she thought it was just the music. But then something like a shout came from behind her.

She straightened and half-turned, and was just reaching down to shut off the sander when a flurry of movement in the house caught her attention. As she flicked the off switch, shock jolted through her when Eddie suddenly appeared at the far end of the kitchen.

His eyes were wide with panic, and blood soaked the front of his shirt as he gripped the edge of the doorframe with one blood-slicked hand.

Jesus! Had he impaled himself on something? She ripped off her goggles and mask, automatically took a step toward him, wanting to help. "Eddie, what—"

"Run," he gasped, and sank to his knees.

She rushed toward him but he shook his head and clamped his hand to the wound in his chest, his expression terrified. And resigned. As if he knew it was too late for him, that he was going to die. "He's...gonna kill you. *Run*."

What? Had someone shot him? Austen recoiled a step, cast a frantic look around. She had to run but she couldn't leave Eddie. "What are you talking about? *Who*?"

"Me."

A scream trapped in her throat as she whirled around to face the silhouette outlined by the bright light flooding through the open doors leading to the deck. Her heart stuttered and she squinted, then the man shifted and she saw the gun in his hand.

Terror raked icy claws at her insides. Her gaze followed that gun as it pointed at her, then trailed up the man's arm...and into a pair of icy blue eyes.

Scott.

Her face prickled as all the blood rushed out of it, and her muscles were taut as wires. "What—" she began, then stopped because her throat closed up.

"You're coming with me," he said in a low, deadly voice, his hand steady on the gun.

Austen stood frozen, too afraid to move, every muscle locked.

"Leave her…'lone," Eddie wheezed behind her.

Scott ignored him, his hate-filled gaze boring into hers. "Come here, bitch," he snarled, motioning impatiently with his free hand, "or I'll shoot you right fucking here and now."

She almost did as he said, almost took a step toward him, but something in her refused to obey. Spinning around, she grabbed the first weapon she could see, a nail gun, then whirled and fired it at him.

He staggered back and clapped a hand to his chest where the nail had driven into his flesh, his cry of pain and rage sent a chill down her spine.

Austen fired again and ran.

He roared in pain. "You're dead, bitch!" He got off a wild shot that punched into the doorframe where her head had just been a split second before, sending up an explosion of splinters.

She veered left and raced for the front door, desperate to get out, to find cover. The extension cord on the nail gun was going to run out soon. She fired again and dropped it as she kept running. Her gaze locked on her truck through the open front door, parked right in front of the porch. She might be able to reach it before he shot her if she was fast enough.

Raw terror exploded through her when she heard his running footsteps on the old wooden floor behind her, almost as loud as the pounding of her heart. Her mind whirled, a thousand things flying through her head all at the same time.

There was no one around to hear her if she screamed for help. Scott was coming after her. He would shoot her, same as he had Eddie.

She had to save herself. Stay alive until help arrived.

She raced through the front door. Her right foot had just landed on the top step when a shot rang out behind her.

****

Wyatt was in a shitty-ass mood by the time he reached the worksite. All that time wasted, and for what? For the past three hours he'd talked to the cops who'd showed up to his place, then answered questions and spoken to detectives down at the police station, with nothing to show for it. He'd been prepared for it, but was still disappointed.

He'd handed over the mask and given them the pictures he'd taken of the footprints outside his back window, but it would be hours yet before they could analyze any of it. The cops said they'd call him if they found anything, but Wyatt had a feeling nothing would come of it.

With no leads and still no idea who had sent those texts, they were at a dead end. And right now, all he wanted was to get back to Austen.

It had only been a few hours since he'd last seen her, but he missed her already and that was a revelation in itself. The only reason he'd let her go into work by herself this morning was because she'd insisted on going, and she wouldn't be alone on site.

After last night he couldn't wait to see her again, wished he could throw her over his shoulder and hide away with her in the cabin for the next week. She was just so damn sweet and kind and sexy, he couldn't help falling for her. If he had his way she'd check out of the motel and stay with him until her house was finished.

Scott's and Eddie's vehicles were parked out front with Austen's when he arrived at the worksite. He picked up the tray of drinks he'd stopped to buy at the café for Austen and the guys, then lifted Grits down from the cab and set him on the ground. The dog turned and raced up the front steps into the house before Wyatt had even shut his door.

Three steps up the front porch, he stopped dead when a terrified female scream ripped through the air, coming from the rear of the house. He'd never heard Austen make that sound before, but he somehow knew it was her. Alarm slammed into him.

"Austen!" The quickest way out back was through the house. He dropped the drinks and charged up the front steps, through the foyer, headed for the kitchen.

Wyatt sucked in a breath and jerked to a halt when he saw Eddie lying facedown in a pool of blood in the kitchen doorway, unmoving. Grits was sniffing at him.

"Jesus Christ," he breathed, and drew his weapon from his waistband. *Austen!* Raw terror flooded him as he jumped over Eddie's body and raced for the deck doors.

She screamed again, from somewhere out in the backyard. The sound was high-pitched, petrified, and it blasted through Wyatt like a frag grenade.

Grits started barking and snarling as he raced through out onto the deck. Wyatt ran after him, noticing the trail of blood staining the drop cloths, leading straight out the doors. Oh, fuck, was she wounded? Outside, Grits was going nuts, snarling and barking hysterically. What the hell was—

His breath caught when he reached the back deck and took in the scene before him.

Off to his left Austen was partially hidden from view in some bushes lining the west side of the yard, and she was trying to fend off someone with a garbage can lid. The man's back was turned to him as he lunged for Austen, a gun in his hand.

She screamed and lashed out with the garbage can lid, striking the assailant in the shoulder and head. Grits was at their feet, snarling and nipping at the man's leg.

The man growled and slashed out a hand at Austen, knocking her weapon away. She whirled to flee but the man shot his arm out and clamped it around her throat, and Wyatt caught a glimpse of his face.

Shock and rage detonated inside him.

Scott. He suppressed the urge to roar in rage and anguish. That bastard. That fucking *bastard*. Wyatt would kill him for daring to go after Austen.

Everything slowed as he raised his weapon.

His pulse thudded in his ears as he took aim, locking on his target just as Scott spun and fired at him.

Chapter SIXTEEN

"*Noooo!*" Austen screamed as the shot exploded from Scott's gun. Heart in her throat, her eyes stayed locked on Wyatt as he dove to the deck and disappeared behind a stack of lumber. She couldn't tell if he'd been hit or not.

Pure rage slammed into her. Baring her teeth, she rammed backward against Scott with all the force she could muster. He grunted and tipped slightly. She seized the opportunity and drove the point of her elbow at his head, intending to smash him in the middle of his lying fucking face.

He dodged the worst of it, her elbow skimming the edge of his cheek. The shift in momentum threw her off balance. She threw out a hand to grab for the nearest branch to keep from falling, and it cost her dearly.

An expression of lethal rage contorting his face, Scott lunged forward to grab her around the throat with his forearm and locked it tight. Grits was barking ferociously just feet from them, charging forward every so often to nip at Scott's legs.

The arm around her throat tightened. Austen choked and struggled, clawing at his skin. Then something hard and cold pressed against her temple and she went dead still as she realized he had the gun to her head.

She was panting, her entire body shaking under a lash of adrenaline and fear. Her eyes darted over to the deck but there was no sign of Wyatt and her heart shattered to think he'd been shot. She needed to get to him, to stop the bleeding—

Grits let out a ferocious snarl and lunged at Scott, sinking sharp teeth into his lower leg.

Scott yelled and kicked the dog off him. Grits cowered. "Get the fuck outta here," Scott growled, and jerked the gun away from her head.

Austen realized his intention and struggled in his hold, tried to ruin his shot. "*No*—"

He fired.

Grits let out a bloodcurdling scream as the bullet hit him, then disappeared into the underbrush.

The tears she'd been holding at bay flooded her eyes as once again Scott shoved the muzzle of the gun against her temple. "Let me go," she choked out, her eyes feeling like they were going to burst from the pressure around her throat.

"Not a fucking chance," he snarled back, dragging her deeper into the bushes. "I'm gonna kill you while Wyatt watches."

"He'll kill you first."

"I don't care if I die, so long as he sees me kill you first."

He was a monster. She could smell blood, could hear Grits's pained cries coming from somewhere nearby. Tears spilled down her cheeks as she focused on the deck, searching for Wyatt.

Scott dragged her to a spot beside an opening in the bushes and she had no choice but to follow. "Why?" she demanded in a strangled voice. Her throat felt raw and bruised from the pressure around it, and her insides were quivering. The will to fight burned bright inside her, fueled by the rage and need for vengeance. She wasn't going to let him kill her, let alone hurt Wyatt by making him watch her die.

"I know you're still alive, Colebrook," Scott called out.

He was breathing hard, his muscles twitching. She could smell his sweat and almost taste his fear, but it was mixed with a terrifying kind of elation and the feel of his erection pressed against her rear turned her stomach.

He was turned on by this. The thrill of the hunt, and the idea of killing her and Wyatt. Sick bastard. She swallowed, frantically thought of what she could do to get out of this.

"Come out like a man and watch what I do to her, you son of a bitch," Scott yelled.

Austen stared at the deck, heart in her throat. Grits was no longer crying, but his agonized whining sliced at her like razors.

"Does she know what happened that day in Afghanistan, Wyatt? Did you tell her what a hero you are before you fucked her on that couch last night?"

Oh God, she was going to be sick.

"Yeah, big-time war hero. A real stud, damn near the Bionic Man!" He paused to draw a breath. "The truth is, you should have died out there with the others. You don't deserve to be here when the rest of them are dead."

Austen's blood turned to ice. If Wyatt was still alive, those words would hurt him more than any bullet wound ever could. "Stop it," she grated out.

Scott jerked his arm against her throat, momentarily cutting off her air, and kept going. "It was your fault,

Wyatt, and you know it. Those Marines are dead because of you. All of them, including Taylor."

Taylor. The grandson of the woman who'd owned this house. What was Scott's connection to Taylor?

"You were his squad leader. He was *your* responsibility. And he was my best friend," he added, his voice cracking. "He should still be here, not you. This house should be *his*, not your goddamn whore's. I should be working for him, not you. But he's dead because of you, and you were the only one who survived. You fucked up and the whole town rallied around you. I didn't do anything wrong and they all turned on me, even my wife. Well, now you're gonna find out the true meaning of suffering, my friend. I'm gonna take her from you while you stand there and watch and there's not a goddamn thing you can do to save her."

Her heart seized when she caught motion at the pile of lumber and then Wyatt appeared, pistol gripped in both hands, his expression icy calm. Relief speared through her when she saw that he wasn't wounded, but she wished he'd stayed behind cover.

The cold look on his face was absolutely terrifying and Scott's cruel words to him pierced her. She was furious that this asshole would blame Wyatt for something he'd had no control over. Wyatt had suffered enough and she wished she could escape Scott's hold long enough to grab the gun and shoot him between the eyes.

"Let her go," Wyatt commanded in a low voice, everything about him radiating cool confidence.

"I don't think so, *sergeant*," Scott sneered.

"I'm not gonna ask again," Wyatt said, and her skin prickled at the menace in his voice.

She was out of time.

For a single heartbeat she stared up at Wyatt through tear-blurred eyes, drinking in the sight of him as she fought past the fear and numbness to unleash the fury burning inside her.

Now.

With a strangled cry of rage, she shot both hands up to lock around the hand holding the gun to her head at the same time as she let her legs go limp. Scott jerked in surprise as her attack caught him off guard, and she wrenched his wrist back and down as hard as she could.

The gun went off, so close to her ear the noise deafened her. He screamed as his wrist snapped, and the gun fell from his hand.

Then the scream cut off suddenly and he went limp. He crashed to the ground, dragging her with him. Terrified, Austen rolled and lunged for the gun. She grabbed it, rolled to her side and aimed it at him.

She stared in shock at the hole in the center of his forehead. Blood trickled down his face, his pale blue eyes half-open and staring vacantly.

The gun fell from her fingers as strong hands gripped her and lifted her against a wide chest. "*Austen.*"

Wyatt's arms banded around her, crushing her to him. She whimpered, clutched at his shoulders as she buried her face in his neck. He set a hand beneath her chin and tipped her face up, his eyes scanning her face anxiously. "Are you okay?"

She managed a nod, everything shaking so badly she couldn't get the words out. Without meaning to she looked over her shoulder, her gaze automatically going to Scott.

"No, don't look." Wyatt took her head in his hands and turned her to face him. Those gorgeous hazel eyes delved into hers, full of concern, and her face crumpled as everything hit home.

"Sweetheart," he groaned, one hand cradling the back of her head as he lifted her and began carrying her out of the bushes.

"N-no," she protested, squirming out of his grip. "Grits."

****

The moment he released her she ran on rubbery legs over to a certain spot in the bushes. Wyatt followed, his stomach hard as a block of concrete. He didn't want to find his dog dead. Just couldn't deal with it on top of everything else. Eddie was already lying dead in the kitchen entryway.

When Austen knelt and pushed the branches away, a pained sound escaped her when she saw Grits. He was lying curled up in a tight ball, his left hindquarters covered in blood. He was panting rapidly, his eyes glazed as he looked up at them, and his heart broke when the end of Grits's tail wagged in recognition.

"Ah, *fuck*," he muttered. Afraid to hurt him more, Wyatt reached in and carefully slid his hands beneath him. Grits let out a sharp yelp and tried to struggle. "No, buddy, just lie still," he said softly as he pulled his dog out.

Wyatt blanched when he saw the full extent of the damage. Before he could say anything Austen was already tugging her shirt over her head and wrapping it around Grits's back end. She darted a glance up at him, still shaking, the adrenaline fading away. "How bad is it?"

Wyatt cradled the dog in his arms, holding him close to his chest. "Bad. We need to get him to the vet's."

Her legs shook as she pushed to her feet. "I'll drive. You keep pressure on him."

"My phone's in my front pocket. Call the cops. Tell them about Eddie." He couldn't stay, not when Grits's life was in danger. If he stayed the cops would never let him leave just to take Grits to the vet. And nobody was dragging him away from his dog.

She pulled it out and dialed, spoke to the 911 operator as they rushed around the side of the house. He marveled at her strength, at how steady she was despite her whole body shaking and her face streaked with tears.

He didn't dare ease up the pressure on Grits's leg. Austen was explaining about Grits, and Wyatt didn't even care that he was leaving the scene of a crime with two dead bodies. He hadn't done anything wrong.

Austen jumped behind the wheel of her truck while he climbed into the passenger seat and she raced down the driveway. "Is he still conscious?"

"Barely." He was so little, and he'd already lost so much blood. Wyatt's shirt and lap were covered in it.

She turned onto the main road and hit the gas, racing toward town. Wyatt could feel himself zoning out, that all-too familiar numbness taking hold. The smell of the blood, Grits's rattling gasps, were just like it had been with Raider.

He didn't even remember arriving at the clinic or rushing Grits inside. He refused to hand Grits over, refused to leave when the vet and her staff rushed to prep Grits for surgery. He stayed glued to the edge of the operating table, crouched down near Grits's head so the dog could see Wyatt.

"Come on, buddy, you gotta hang in there." His voice was rough as sandpaper.

A crushing sense of guilt smothered him. This dog had suffered at the hands of a human before. Wyatt was supposed to have been his second chance, his fresh start. Instead he was fighting for his life because a fellow veteran who Wyatt had trusted had shot him, killed Eddie, and had been about to kill Austen.

Staring down into Grits's dazed brown eyes, he was sucked back in time to those moments when he'd been holding Raider, looking into her eyes and begging her to hold on right before she'd died in his arms. He clenched his teeth together and swallowed as the acidic grief burned in his chest.

"Sir, I really need you to clear out of here so my staff and I can get to work," the vet told him, her tone making it a command rather than a request.

Wyatt looked up at her, feeling tortured. "I can't leave him."

The vet's eyes softened with sympathy. "Best way you can help him is to let us get started. We'll let you know the prognosis as soon as we can."

Swallowing, Wyatt stroked a hand over Grits's head and neck. His fur was so damn soft, the white all matted and rusty-colored with blood. "I'll be right outside," he promised him, then forced his feet to turn him around and take him out to the waiting room.

Austen was there. She jumped out of her seat, dressed in a scrubs top someone at the clinic must have given her. Her eyes were worried, her face pale and stained with tears. "How is he?"

"Bad," was all he could manage before the lump in his throat choked him.

Austen's expression filled with empathy and tenderness as she reached for him.

Wyatt went into her arms without a second's hesitation, burying his face in her throat as he slid his arms around her and held her as tight as he could without hurting her.

She kissed his temple and stroked the back of his head as she whispered to him. "He's got such a big heart, Wyatt, and he loves you. He'll fight his way through this, just wait and see."

Wyatt nodded because he didn't see the point in arguing and he didn't want to crush her hopes by telling her it wasn't going to happen. And it wasn't just Grits that had him so emotional. Here Austen was, trying to comfort him when she'd had a gun to her head less than an hour ago. It killed him.

He crushed her to him and he held on tight. She was his anchor, the only thing stopping him from falling to pieces right here in the middle of the veterinary office.

He dimly realized he was breathing too fast, that he was rapidly losing control. He fought back the flood of tears that threatened to escape, muscling them back by sheer force of will. Austen was traumatized enough and he wasn't going to be a selfish asshole by unloading all his bullshit baggage on her after what she'd just gone through.

She didn't speak. Just like in the aftermath of his nightmare last night, she simply held him, allowed him to gain control and find his footing again. And when he could breathe again, when his heart no longer felt like it would explode, he raised his head and took her face between his hands so he could look into her eyes.

That beautiful silver gaze met his, and he felt his heart free-fall. "I love you," he blurted.

Her eyes widened in surprise but then a smile flickered at the edges of her mouth. "I love you too."

Elation and relief filled him. "I was so fucking scared when I saw him holding that gun to your head."

She grimaced and for a second he felt bad about saying anything, but hell, he wanted her to know how much she meant to him. "Me too."

He stroked his thumbs across her cheeks, savoring the softness as he tried to wipe the traces of her tears away. She'd been through too much, before with losing her fiancé and leaving everything she knew and loved behind to start a new life, then today, nearly losing that life.

It shook him. "I didn't care if I died so long as you were safe. That's all that mattered to me." It was important to him that she understood that.

"If you'd died, I would have anyway," she whispered, and he recognized the ghosts of past grief in her eyes. "That would have ended me."

"No," he said, shaking his head. "You're so much stronger than you even realize. You saved yourself today by taking action, all I did was pull the trigger. And then you drove me here, half-naked, after just being held at gunpoint and seeing two men die because you wanted to save Grits. So yeah, I love you. And I would have died to protect you without thinking twice about it."

She closed her eyes and leaned her forehead against his, their noses touching. "Well let's just be glad it didn't come to that."

Yeah, no kidding.

Taking her hand, Wyatt led her over to the row of chairs in the waiting room and pulled her into his lap. He was covered in blood but he knew Austen wouldn't care. All that mattered was being able to touch her and hold her, offer her comfort and reassure himself that she was still alive.

About twenty minutes later the operating room door opened and the vet stepped out. Wyatt stiffened, his stomach shriveling into a tight, aching ball.

"We got a transfusion into him and he seems stable for the moment. But I can't save his leg. Not in a way that would allow him to walk without pain again."

Wyatt's heart had swelled at the first bit of news, but the second bit made it plummet. "So what do you want to do?" he asked.

"I recommend amputation. It's less risky for him in the short term, and much kinder in the long run. There's no guarantee that he'll pull out of this surgery though. He lost over half his blood volume."

Wyatt nodded slowly. "Okay. Whatever you need to do."

"It's an expensive procedure, on top of the transfusion and—"

"I don't care what it costs." He'd sell his damn truck to pay for the bill if he had to.

The vet offered an encouraging smile. "I'll get my staff to draw up the consent forms. He should be out of surgery within the hour, and of course we'll want to keep him for a few days. If you want to go home and clean up, we can call you when he's in recovery."

"I'll stay." He wasn't going until Grits was out of surgery. And he didn't bother telling the vet that they'd rushed here from a murder scene, after Wyatt had killed the gunman.

Soon enough he'd have to face everything that had happened back at the house. The cops were probably on their way here to talk to them. He and Austen would be interviewed separately, and there'd be a lot of other steps to take care of before they'd be allowed to go home.

He looked at Austen, who nodded and shifted her gaze to the doctor. "We're both staying."

Chapter SEVENTEEN

P iper stopped in the act of putting a lid on her vanilla latte and frowned as she looked out the café's front windows. The wail of the sirens coming down Main Street grew louder, and seconds later, two more patrol cars zipped past. The fifth and sixth ones she'd seen go by since she'd entered the café a few minutes ago. Whatever was going on, it had to be bad.

Hurrying out the door, she climbed in her car and drove to the Miller place, careful to take the turns slow so that the plate of brownies and the lemon-sour cream pie balanced on the passenger seat didn't fall over. She'd made the pie last night and pulled the brownies from the oven less than forty minutes ago, before she'd jumped in the shower, so they were still warm. She hoped Austen and Wyatt liked them.

But when she turned down the street to the Miller place, a ball of dread formed in the pit of her stomach when she saw all the emergency vehicles blocking the driveway.

Had someone been hurt on the job site? Worry gnawing at her, she parked a half block away and crossed the street. All the cops knew her, since she'd been married to the former sheriff. Thankfully most of them didn't hold that against her.

One of the most senior deputies, Frank, saw her coming and met her on the sidewalk. "Everything okay?" she asked, casting a worried look over the fence into the front yard.

"No, I'm afraid not."

Piper jerked her attention back to him, the dread growing stronger. "Why, what's wrong?"

"Can't give details right now, but it's serious. Medical examiner is on his way."

What? Someone had been *murdered*? She blanched. "Are Wyatt and Austen okay?" She didn't know any of the others working on site.

"I don't know who was involved. Sorry."

Oh my God. Wyatt had told her that someone had sent him threatening texts. And then Greg had showed up and threatened him at his house.

A sick feeling permeated her. Was Frank hiding that Greg was behind this? Had her ex actually lost it completely and hunted Wyatt down, then killed him in cold blood out of some insane notion of jealousy?

No. No, he wouldn't.

But what if he *had*?

Heart pounding, she pushed past Frank, intent on getting through the barricade and up the driveway so she could see what the hell was going on.

He caught her upper arm and turned her around, his grip gentle but firm. "I can't let you go in there, Piper."

"Please just tell me if they're okay," she pleaded, half frantic. "They're my friends."

"I honestly don't know. I'm sorry, but I can't let you in." His expression told her he felt badly. "Is there anyone I can call for you?"

Ignoring the offer, she dug out her own phone and dialed Wyatt. The ringtone droned in her ear, grating on her tautly stretched nerves. Three rings later, his voicemail picked up. "Shit," she whispered, starting to tremble as the fear hit her. She dialed Austen next, and same thing.

"No, no," she muttered, and out of desperation dialed Easton's number. He didn't answer either.

She stepped past Frank, who followed her like a bloodhound as she rushed to the tape blocking off the end of the driveway. Casting a frantic look down it, she spotted Wyatt's truck parked out front. Nausea churned in her stomach. *Oh my God...*

On wobbly legs she turned around and ran back to her car, dialing Wyatt once more before she pulled away from the curb and raced back toward town. She got his voicemail again. Swallowing hard, she sped down Main Street and out into the countryside, on autopilot as she headed for the Colebrook place.

By the time she arrived at the farmhouse she was on the verge of tears. Easton's truck was parked out front. She bounded up the front steps and banged on the door, about to lose it. Quick footsteps sounded from inside and then the door swung open to reveal Easton standing there, bare-chested.

"Something bad's happened at Austen's place," she blurted, almost panting because her breathing was so choppy. "I went there, but the on-duty cops wouldn't let me in, and then I called Wyatt's and Austen's phones but they didn't answer—"

"They're okay," he said quietly.

She stopped, blinked at him as his words penetrated, a wave of relief slamming over her. "How do you know?"

"Wyatt called me. He and Austen are both okay."

"One of the cops said the medical examiner was en route."

Easton nodded, his brown eyes somber. "Two people died."

She swallowed. "Who?"

"Two guys on the crew."

Oh, man, how awful. "Did Wyatt say what happened?" she asked carefully, dreading his answer. If Greg had done this, she didn't know what she'd do.

"Yeah."

That he didn't just tell her spiked her anxiety. "What?" she demanded, about to snap. "Why won't you tell me?"

Easton sighed and scrubbed a hand over his face, then reached for her hand and pulled her inside. "Come sit down," he said, leading her into the front parlor. "You look pale."

She sank onto the sofa while Easton sat on the coffee table in front of her, resting his elbows on his knees and it was unsettling to realize she was having a hard time keeping her eyes on his face when all those chiseled muscles were on display a mere foot-and-a-half away.

"One of Wyatt's guys killed one of the others, and attacked Austen." He paused. "It was Scott."

She stared at him, aghast. "The guy who worked here on the farm?"

Easton nodded. "Apparently he had a grudge against Wyatt for what happened to Taylor over in Afghanistan. He wanted to even the score by killing Austen in front of Wyatt."

"Oh my God," she whispered, horrified. It was so sick and wrong.

"Yeah. I'm not clear on the details yet, but Wyatt shot him. He's dead."

"Good."

One side of Easton's mouth tipped up at her response, and she struggled to ignore just how gorgeous he was. "That's what I said."

Shuffling footsteps on the staircase made her look over and Mr. C came into view.

"Piper," he acknowledged as he headed down the remaining stairs. "You hear the news?"

"Just now. You okay?" How awful, to find out one of the men he'd hired had done this.

"Wyatt and Austen are okay, so yes, I'm fine."

Piper looked back at Easton. "Are you guys heading out to meet Wyatt?"

He nodded. "They're at the vet clinic."

"What? Why?"

He grimaced and reached out to take her hands. "Grits was shot."

She gasped, one hand flying to her chest. "No!"

He nodded. "Looks like he's going to lose one of his back legs."

"That son of a bitch," she fumed, shoving to her feet. Killing one of his coworkers, threatening Austen, and then shooting an innocent little dog? She hoped he was burning in hell right now.

Easton rose and rubbed his hands over her upper arms, but the soothing touch did nothing to calm her down. "Wyatt and Austen are down at the clinic. They've gotta talk to the cops after, and Wyatt didn't want Grits to be alone so he asked me to come stay with him while he's in recovery."

"Oh, but... Why wouldn't he call me to do that?" Maybe it was stupid to feel hurt by that, but she'd been the one to bring the dog to him in the first place. Wyatt knew how much she loved animals, and how much she cared about him and his family.

"He didn't want to upset you," Easton said, still rubbing her arms. For some reason his touch sent distracting and unwanted tingles racing over her skin.

Unsettled by her body's reaction, she stepped back, out of reach, and cleared her throat. This was the first time she'd ever felt like an outsider with them. Even through Wyatt's long rehab once he'd come home from the hospital, his family had allowed her to be here in the thick of things. They'd let her help them all, leaned on her for support. "I was heading over to Austen's place to drop off some treats I made. They're in the car. Can I leave them in the cabin?"

"Of course."

She turned and headed for the front door, mind whirling, a flurry of emotions pushing her precariously close to tears. Easton followed her out and she wished he hadn't. She could use a few minutes alone to compose herself.

He was right behind her when she opened the front passenger door and saw the mess on the seat. "Oh no…"

She'd been in such a rush to get here, she hadn't even thought about the baking during the turns. Brownies and crumbs were strewn all over the seat, and some pie filling had smeared on the center armrest where the plastic wrap had come undone and the pie had smashed against it.

Easton stuck his head in to take a look. "Still looks good to me," he said, and began scooping the fallen brownies back onto the paper plate she'd stacked them on.

Piper swallowed, struggling against tears, but couldn't quite hold back a sniffle as she dealt with the pie.

"Hey," Easton murmured, setting the plate down and taking her by the shoulders. She tensed and resisted turning around to face him, afraid she'd break down, but he was insistent.

Blinking up at him as the unwelcome tears formed, her voice wobbled. "I just wanted to take them some brownies," she whispered, all her normal control deserting her.

He grinned and pulled her into a hug—against his hard, bare chest. "That was real nice of you. They smell amazing, as always," he said, his arms so warm and solid around her. And he smelled way better than the brownies.

"They're ruined," she said, feeling miserable. It was weird and creepy, her suddenly being aware of Wyatt's little brother in a physical way. She'd be mortified if he ever found out, and being held to his naked chest was torture.

"They're not," he soothed.

Piper squeezed her eyes shut and blurted out the truth she'd been holding back. "I was afraid it was Greg." She paused a beat, unable to look at him because she felt so ashamed that she'd ever married her ex. "When I heard the medical examiner was coming, that's what I thought. That maybe Greg had gone after Wyatt at the house."

"Hey," he said again, waiting until she finally looked at him before continuing. "It wasn't, but it doesn't make you a bad person for wondering that. Greg has serious issues. And that's not your fault either. You know that, right? You're not responsible for his actions and decisions."

She lowered her gaze to stare down at his boots. "I know."

"Good." He drew her close again, one hand on the back of her head, pressing her cheek to his bare shoulder.

This time Piper sighed and allowed herself to relax into his embrace. She'd had no one to lean on for so long. Not this way, and even if Easton was Wyatt's little brother, he still felt damn good.

Soaking up his offer of comfort like a thirsty sponge, her hands crept up his back to rest against his shoulder blades. Warm, smooth skin met her palms, powerful muscles bunching beneath them. Arousal sparked throughout her body, potent and forbidden, making her nipples tighten.

Wyatt's little brother, she reminded herself, horrified by the leap of need that was getting harder and harder to ignore. She pulled out of his embrace, desperate for space and ashamed of her reaction.

"Hell, if Wyatt doesn't want 'em, I'll eat 'em. You know I love your baking," Easton said.

She shook her head. "They're for him and Austen. I'll make you your own."

"Yeah? Better do it soon, then, 'cuz I'm only here for a couple more days."

She searched his face. "You're leaving again already?" He usually had at least a week or two off in between missions before he had to go back to work.

He nodded, and something she'd never seen before moved in his warm brown eyes. Yearning? And a weariness that made her want to wrap him up in her arms and never let go. "Yeah, already."

"Where are you going this time?" She hated that his job was so dangerous, but he was even more of an adrenaline junkie than their middle brother Brody was, and loved living life on the edge. He said it made him feel alive.

"Who knows? Wherever they need us to stomp out the drug trade the most this week," he said, his tone teasing but again she could see that unfamiliar, timeworn look in his eyes. Then he cocked his head and gave her one of his trademark grins that transformed his expression. "You all right now?"

For just a moment the sheer male beauty of him stunned her. She blinked and cleared her suddenly dry throat. "Yes."

"Let's take this over and put it in the fridge for them," he said, releasing her to pick up the plate of brownies. "After the shit day they've had, I'm sure they'll appreciate some homemade goodies."

Piper bent to gather what was left of the pie. When she straightened she could have sworn she caught him staring at her ass, but then he walked away, heading for the cabin without a backward glance and she told herself she had to have imagined it.

Because if she hadn't, she didn't know what the hell to make of it.

Feeling totally off balance, she followed him over to the cabin and put the pie in the fridge while he set the brownies on the table.

"This one's pretty smashed up," he commented, picking one off the top. "I should probably eat it, to make the presentation better."

She laughed softly. "Like there was ever any doubt."

He took a huge bite and chewed, rolled his eyes heavenward as a low moan spilled from his lips. "So good."

Something eased inside her and she smiled, trying to ignore what the sound of that moan did to her. One of her greatest pleasures was watching people enjoy her baking. "I'm glad. Well, I guess I should let you and your dad get to the vet's."

He walked her out to her car, polishing off the rest of the brownie. "You okay to drive?"

"Oh yeah, I'm fine." Since leaving Greg she'd been on a mission to reinvent herself. She was strong and independent, didn't want anyone to think she was weak, least of all Easton and his family.

"You sure look fine," he said with an appreciative grin meant to raise her spirits.

Was he flirting with her? Or just teasing, as usual? Given how weird things had been this afternoon, she couldn't tell for certain. There was no way he was attracted to her. He was so hard to read but she and everyone else in Sugar Hollow knew he was never short of female company. Why would he ever be interested in her when he could have any woman he wanted, and she had also once dated his eldest brother? Ick.

He put her in her car, waited while she lowered the window and bent to rest his stacked, corded forearms against the lower window frame. His gaze searched hers, warm and steady. So different from the wild child of the Colebrook family she'd always seen him as. "You sure you're all right? I can drive you home on the way to the vet's and one of us can drop your car off later."

"No, I'm fine." She'd gotten in the habit of turning down offers of help after leaving Greg. Lord knew she'd made some shitty decisions in her life and paid dearly for them, but she was starting to crawl her way out of the pit she'd dug for herself. "You guys get going. Tell them I said hi, and please keep me updated on Grits. If they need anything, tell them to call." She hoped they'd ask her. They were like family to her.

"I will." He straightened, and she couldn't help but admire his naked torso as he rose to his full height. Just over six feet, a shade less than Brody, and just as muscular. "I'm still gonna get my own brownies, right?"

Stop staring, pervert. She shot him a smile. "Yes, you'll still get your own brownies."

He grinned. "Thanks, sweet thing, you're the best." He stepped away. "Drive safely."

For a long moment Piper sat there and watched his gorgeous, masculine form walk back toward the house, shocked at the aching sense of longing growing inside her.

Horrified, she yanked her gaze away and started the engine, shaking her head at herself. "What the hell is *wrong* with you?" she muttered, and took off down the driveway.

Her disturbing reaction to Easton today only solidified what she'd already known for a long time now. The sooner she left Sugar Hollow and everything in it behind her, the better.

Chapter EIGHTEEN

O ne hand braced on the wall, Wyatt stood in the shower and let the hot water beat down on his head and shoulders. It was only one in the afternoon and he was weary to the bone, felt as though he hadn't slept in days.

He'd stayed at the vet clinic until Grits had come out of surgery, had refused to leave until they let him see his dog. The sight of him lying there all drugged up with a bandage wrapped around the stump where his back lower leg had once been had choked Wyatt up.

Only thing that made leaving him bearable was knowing Easton was there with him. Wyatt had wanted to come back and stay the night at the clinic but Easton had flat out refused, telling him that Austen needed him more.

It wasn't often that he took advice from his wild little brother, but in this case, Easton was right.

The cops had come to the vet clinic, and taken him and Austen back to the job site. It hadn't been easy for him to go there, but he knew it had been a hell of a lot harder on her. She was a civilian, had never been in combat, and had never been exposed to that kind of violence before. Thankfully both bodies had been removed before they'd arrived. The lead detective had separated them to question them individually and get their statements, walking them both through the chain of events that had resulted in Wyatt killing Scott.

Once that was done, they'd had to go down to the police station for more paperwork, and fingerprinting. By the time he'd been allowed to see Austen again she'd looked drawn and exhausted.

She'd met him out front of the interview room and reached for him the moment she walked out into the hall. After stopping by her motel to pick up a change of clothes they'd come back here to clean up and change and Austen had called her mom to tell her what had happened.

God knew he could use these few minutes alone, to regroup. There was so much static going on in his head, it was slowly driving him insane.

He soaped himself, scrubbing away the blood staining his skin, the sight and smell of it turning his stomach. It wasn't even human blood, but that didn't matter. That unmistakable smell was permanently burned into his psyche and would always trigger memories from that terrible day in Afghanistan.

And then Scott's poisonous words replayed in his mind. He squeezed his eyes shut and shook his head, fighting to make it stop. Austen needed him—he didn't have time to dwell on his own shit.

Clean and dressed, he walked out into the kitchen to find her at the counter. Her back was to him, giving him a perfect view of her tight ass in her yoga pants, her smooth, bare arms exposed by the long tank she wore.

She'd been so strong through this whole thing. Maybe it was her training and experience as a first responder, but that strength, considering what had happened, astounded him. She was one hell of an amazing woman.

She tossed a smile at him over her shoulder, her curls brushing her cheek, but it didn't dispel the fatigue he could read in her eyes. "I pulled out the goodies Piper left us," she said, handing him a plate. "Brownies and some kind of lemon cream pie."

"Aw, yeah," he murmured in satisfaction, and picked up the brownie to take a bite. Bless Piper. "Just what the doctor ordered."

Austen murmured in agreement as she forked up a bite of the pie and let out a soft moan. "Oh, man, this is good. Did she make this herself?"

"Mmhmm. That girl loves to bake."

"Well she's damn good at it. Wanna go eat out on the back porch?"

"Sure."

They sat on the porch swing and devoured the dessert together. He set his empty plate on the table in front of them, then ran a hand over Austen's hair, the curls clinging to his fingers. "You doing okay?"

She nodded. "I think so." Her gaze sought his. "You?"

"Yeah." Way better than he would have been without her here. He curled his arm around her shoulders and drew her into his body.

She snuggled into him with a sigh, tucking her feet beneath her as he used his left foot to gently rock the porch swing. Through the large screen panels in front of them, horses grazed on the lush green pastures beyond the white-painted fence.

He still couldn't believe Scott would betray him this way, after all Wyatt had done for him. Given him a steady job here on the farm, overlooking his PTSD issues. Wyatt knew full well how it felt to be discriminated against and how hard it was for a combat veteran to reintegrate back into civilian life and society after they'd experienced so many horrific things while serving their country.

Wyatt didn't know if he could forgive himself for screwing up so badly.

"I love how quiet it is back here," Austen murmured. "I needed this. Thanks for bringing me back here."

"No way in hell was I taking you back to that motel." He stroked her hair again, loving the bouncy texture. "I'd love for you to stay here with me instead, for however long you want."

"That's a very open-ended offer. What if you get sick of me after a couple weeks?"

He snorted. "Not gonna happen."

"What if I'm a total slob and drive you nuts?"

Things had moved fast between them, but he knew what he wanted, and it was her. "You aren't. I've seen your motel room and the way you organize things at the job site. It'll be fine."

Her lips twitched. "Well then, I just might take you up on that offer. Could be a long time before we finish the house, though. You sure you're up for it?"

"You sure you're ready to go back there?" Right now it was a crime scene, so they might not be able to go back by Monday morning.

She blinked at him. "What, to the house? Of course I am! I'm not letting that piece of shit take my dream from me. To hell with that. I'm finishing that house, come hell or high water."

God, he loved that fierce little scowl on her face. "You don't want to take some time to think about it?"

"What's to think about? I'm all in, spent my life's savings and John's life insurance settlement on this. No way I'm walking away. I'll take a couple days off just to let things…settle, then get back at it Monday morning." She eyed him, looking concerned. "Why, are you having second thoughts?"

He shook his head, even though he was having second thoughts about a lot of things. But not about her. He'd never felt so certain of anything than he did of him and Austen.

"Good," she said with a decisive nod. "Monday it is."

In answer he squeezed her shoulder and turned his head to stare out at the rolling pasture. He'd been concerned about coming back here with her at first after leaving her motel, worried that it might trigger something because Scott had been here last night. She didn't seem upset about that and he was relieved because this was his safe haven and he wasn't going to let that bastard take it from him.

The peace and quiet here was a godsend. He had at least a dozen voice messages on his phone from Brody, Charlie and Piper, but he was too emotionally drained to call them back tonight. Maybe in the morning, after he'd gone to see Grits.

Hell, he didn't know if he was ready to go back to the job site and face everything, but if Austen could then he would too. It not only reminded him of Taylor now, but of seeing Scott holding that gun to Austen's head. And then there was poor Grits, who was still at the clinic while Easton stood watch.

He exhaled deeply and focused on the now. As the quiet surrounded them and he gazed out at the grazing horses in the distance, he got lost in his own head. Scott was dead. The threat was over for him and Austen, but

Wyatt still blamed himself for what had happened. "I never saw it coming," he said finally.

Austen lifted her head from his shoulder to look at him. "Scott?"

He nodded, jaw tight, hating even the sound of that fucker's name. "I shouldn't have hired him. I shouldn't have trusted him."

"Wyatt, it wasn't your fault. The toxicology reports will prove he was higher than a kite when everything happened this morning. He duped everyone, gave no signs that you could have picked up on. You can't blame yourself."

Hell yes he could. He should have seen this coming. Should have realized Scott was unstable and acted sooner. Dammit, he should have been able to prevent what had happened this morning.

Just like his squad, he'd let Austen down. That was the hardest part to swallow, apart from knowing that Eddie was dead, and poor little Grits had lost a leg today because of Wyatt's bad judgment. Austen had almost paid the price with her life. He couldn't take that.

Needing to feel her up against him, he wrapped both his arms around her and held on tight. She scooted into his lap and cuddled in close, easing the worst of the ache in the center of his chest.

She was too good for him. He was nothing but a scarred-up, wounded combat vet who would never be the man he'd once been. He'd caused so much grief and death and suffering to those who depended on him.

It had been his idea to hire Scott and the other veterans in the first place. He'd insisted upon it. And because of that Austen had nearly died and he'd placed his brother and father at risk when Scott had come skulking around here last night.

Scott may have been high and crazy this morning, but his accusations had been bang on. Wyatt didn't deserve to be here. Taylor and the other Marines had been his responsibility. They'd died under his command, on his watch. There was no excuse, no sugar-coating that.

Wyatt buried his face in Austen's hair and let out a shuddering breath, feeling like he was about to crack apart. Even though he knew he didn't deserve her, there was no way he could let her go. Not now. Not ever.

As though she sensed just how close he was to coming unglued, Austen took his face in her hands. He shook his head, tried to pull away but she was having none of it. "Wyatt, look at me," she said, her voice firm.

Sucking in a deep breath, he swallowed past the lump in his throat and met her gaze. She stared back at him unflinchingly, her expression fierce.

"Don't you dare listen to a word he said to you," she demanded. "What happened over there was not your fault, do you hear me? It was the enemy's fault, no one else's. I know what kind of man you are, and I know you did everything humanly possible to protect them and Raider." Her eyes softened, the tenderness there making him blink fast to stop the tears from forming. "And I also know you would have traded places with any of the guys you lost that day."

He nodded, once again blown away by her perception. God, he would have done that in a heartbeat if it could have saved one of his Marines.

"But I'm so thankful that you survived and came home again," she went on. "You're alive and so am I, thanks to you."

He made a scoffing sound. "He was going to kill you because of me," he forced out, his voice like gravel, the lump in his throat so huge it was all he could do to breathe past it.

"But he didn't, because you saved me. *You* did that, Wyatt, no one else. It was awful and just thinking about it scares me to death, but it's over now, and we have each other." Her thumbs stroked at the stubble on his cheeks. "We're both alive and we should be celebrating that, not feeling guilty about it. It's what your guys and my fiancé would have wanted. We owe it to them to live life to the fullest, don't you think?"

He managed a nod. He owed those fallen Marines everything, and in a way he owed John too. John wasn't here to love and honor and cherish Austen, but Wyatt was. He didn't take that responsibility lightly, and would make sure he looked after her.

Austen gave him a tender smile that almost shattered him. "I love you. I never expected to fall for anyone again, but then I found you—or you found me, on my front porch," she teased. "I refuse to let you pull away now, because I need you and I want you in my life. Bottom line, I'm not letting you go, so just deal with it."

Her words pierced the most deeply buried part of him, cracking him wide open. He'd lived with the guilt for so long, that pain had been far worse than anything he'd endured physically. "I need you too," he said in a rough whisper as his eyes filled up. "And I love you so goddamn much I don't even know what to do with it." It would kill him if he lost her.

Her smile widened and he could see the joy sparkling in those pretty silver eyes as she brushed the tears away before they could fall. "You do this," she told him softly, then covered his lips with hers. "And this," she added, wrapping her arms around his back and squeezing hard, her face nestled in the curve of his neck. "Life and love are precious. When you find someone worthy of giving your heart to, you hold onto them and never let go."

Wyatt crushed her to him, pressing his face into her scented curls. "I won't let you go," he promised, and the moment he said the words the aching pressure in his

208

chest disappeared. For the first time in hours—no, years—he felt like he could finally breathe again.

Austen was right. Life wasn't perfect, but he had it better than a lot of people on this earth. It was high time he dropped the burden of guilt he'd been carrying on his shoulders for so long, and start savoring every moment he had left.

With Austen as the prize, there was no way he was failing that mission.

Epilogue

Two months later

Austen could barely contain her excitement as she waited at the airport for Wyatt to pick her up. This was a big day.

She'd spent two weeks down in Mississippi visiting her mom, and the last four days in Philly, catching up with old friends. Though her mom hadn't met Wyatt in person yet, she was totally in love with him based on the things Austen had told her about him, and their few phone conversations.

While in Philly she'd also visited John's grave. She'd sat there on the grass before his headstone and told him all about her move to Sugar Hollow and what had happened there.

Mostly she'd talked about Wyatt, and how much John would have liked and respected him. She'd always love John, but she wasn't done living yet and had been lucky to fall in love again with a man like Wyatt. In her heart she knew John would be happy for her.

Wheeling her suitcase away from the luggage carousel, she headed for the automatic doors at the end of the baggage claim area. The doors swished open and her heart leapt when Wyatt appeared, wearing a black Stetson, a deep blue button-down shirt and jeans.

And at his side trotted Grits, using his new artificial leg.

The little guy's gait wasn't perfect, but just the sight of him walking with his new prosthetic and his tail wagging turned her to mush. Wyatt had kept her updated with the dog's progress during her trip and sent pictures, but this was the first time she'd seen him in person since he'd gotten his new leg.

A wide smile split her face and she rushed toward them. "Look at you guys!"

Wyatt grinned back and caught her to him with one powerful arm, swooping down to crush his mouth to hers.

I'm finally home, she thought to herself, kissing him back just as hard. It had been too long since she'd felt his arms around her and his mouth on hers.

She was a little breathless when he finally raised his head, his hazel eyes warm. "Miss us?"

"Terribly." She planted another kiss on his tempting lips then bent down to greet Grits. "Hey, little man, look at you! You look so awesome." She ruffled his ears, shot a smile up at Wyatt. "You're like a matching set now."

"Kinda, yeah," he answered, his smile full of pride. "He's doing great. We've been going to the pool four times a week to swim, and his muscle's building up nicely. His prosthesis is fitting really well. The vet's thrilled so far."

"We're so proud of you, Grits," she told him, laughing when he jumped up to rest his front paws on her chest and lick her like crazy.

Less than an hour later they reached Sugar Hollow. But rather than turn right to head toward his place, he turned left. "Where are we going?"

"Don't you wanna see the progress I've made on the house?"

"Well yeah, but I thought—"

"Trust me, you wanna see it," he said.

She'd left the project in his capable hands while she went on holiday. In the aftermath of the attack the entire town had been abuzz with what had happened. The rest of Wyatt's crew had been horrified about Scott. Wyatt had insisted upon new background checks for all the remaining workers, and everyone had checked out just fine. "Okay."

Her heart beat a little faster when he turned down the driveway. It was still hard to come here and be reminded of what had happened, but she was determined to get past it and hoped that over time it would fade completely. She'd sunk her heart and soul into this house, into her life, and she'd be damned if she let Scott—may he be repeatedly burning in hell—take that from her.

"Wait, I need you to put this on first," Wyatt said, drawing a blindfold from his pocket.

She lifted an eyebrow. "Are we planning to christen one of the rooms with some kinky bondage sex?"

He cracked a laugh. "Later. I can't wait for you to see this." He tied it over her eyes and took her hand. "Small steps. I'll lead you through."

Grits hobbled up the front steps with them, and the familiar scents of sawdust and wood stain greeted her when Wyatt opened the front door. "Come on through," he said, and the excitement in his tone told her he was looking forward to her reaction.

She allowed him to lead her through to the kitchen.

"Ready?" he asked.

"Ready."

He pulled off the blindfold, and when her eyes adjusted to the sudden brightness she let out a gasp, both hands flying up to cover her mouth. She wasn't sure how it was possible in such a short amount of time, but the kitchen was finished. "Oh my God, it's beautiful!"

With a sense of wonder and pride she strode forward to run her hands over the granite counters, smoothed her fingertips over the cabinets she'd worked so hard on. The white apron-front farmhouse sink was installed, along with stainless steel appliances and the faucet she'd picked out. "Oh, Wyatt." She was speechless.

He stepped up behind her and wrapped his arms around her waist, setting his chin on the top of her shoulder. She loved how they fit together so easily, like two pieces of a puzzle. "Like it?"

"I love it. I love *you*," she added, turning to hug him. "God, you must have worked like a dog to get this done while I was away. How did you manage it?"

"Called in a few favors. There's more. Come see upstairs."

More? He took her hand and led her upstairs, the sound of Grits's new foot on the treads putting a bittersweet smile on her face.

Wyatt stopped outside the master suite with his free hand on the knob, the anticipation on his face contagious. "Ready?"

"Yes." She was practically dancing in place. "Let me see."

He swung the door open and stepped back to let her through.

"Oh! Ohhhhhh," she breathed, hands on her cheeks as she took it all in. She wasn't sure how he'd managed it, but the entire room was finished.

The walls were a soft buttercream, the moldings and baseboards painted bright white. A four-poster bed graced the largest wall, covered in a sumptuous bedspread. Two night tables with matching lamps flanked it, and a gorgeous crystal chandelier hung from the ceiling. Even the fireplace and mantel were all done, a log set already placed inside, waiting to be lit.

"Take a look in the bathroom," he urged from behind her.

Near tears, she walked through into the master bathroom, and bit her lip. Everything was completed in here too. New tile floor, double vanity, new cabinets, a pretty crystal chandelier…every last detail was done the way she'd wanted, right down to the claw foot tub he must have had refinished during her trip.

"It's perfect," she whispered in a choked voice as the tears began to fall.

With a low chuckle Wyatt came up and drew her into his arms, kissing her lightly. "I'm glad you're happy with it."

"Happy? Oh my God, that's not even close to the right word. It's amazing, Wyatt. Truly, unbelievably amazing."

"The decorative stuff is all Piper. I just oversaw the construction and did a few projects here and there."

She shook her head at him, wanting to cry, it meant so much to her. "You're unreal. You know that?"

"I know how much you wanted to get the kitchen and master suite done, so you could move in. I wanted to have that much done by the time you got back."

And he'd managed to do all that on top of helping his dad with the farm and taking Grits back and forth to all his appointments. She pushed back to gaze up into his eyes. This was beyond any gift she could ever imagine. "Thank you."

"You're welcome." His grin told her that her reaction and thanks were all he needed. God, she loved him.

"But I only want to move in if you move in with me. Since it's your house too."

He looked surprised by that. "You sure?"

"Yes, I'm sure! I thought about it a lot while I was away. I could never sell this place, and I want it to be your home too." She shot him a saucy grin. "So. Wanna be roomies?"

"Wanna get married?"

What? She stopped and stared up at him, shocked. They hadn't really talked about this and she'd never expected Wyatt to ask her so soon. He grimaced and laughed at himself. "That wasn't even close to how I planned to ask you. Hold on."

Dropping to one knee, he reached into his pocket and pulled out a square velvet box. Then he shot a look at Grits. "Grits."

The dog's floppy ears perked up and he wagged his tail.

"Sit."

Grits sat.

"Paw. Just like we rehearsed."

Oh my God, they'd rehearsed this? Austen was torn between tears and laughter. They were too damn adorable.

Grits lifted one white front paw in the air and waved it up and down, his big brown eyes staring up at her.

Wyatt took his cue. He opened the ring box to reveal a round diamond ring that sparkled in the light. "Austen, will you make us the happiest man and dog in the world and be my wife?"

Grits gazed up at her in encouragement, paw still raised, his tail swishing back and forth on the glossy floorboards.

There was no question that she wanted to spend the rest of her life with this sexy, endearing man. Austen dropped to her knees and flung her arms around Wyatt's neck. "Yes!" Wyatt hugged her to him as she sought his lips with hers.

A second later, little paws landed on her left thigh and then a wet tongue was licking at her cheek. She laughed and let go of Wyatt long enough to scoop Grits up into her arms. "This means I get to be your mama for real," she told him, grinning when he licked her chin, his entire body wiggling with the force of his wagging tail.

"Upstaged by a dog during the most important moment of my life," Wyatt muttered, his eyes warm with amusement.

"I'll make it up to you right now," Austen promised, setting the dog down to clasp her arms around his neck. "Now slide that ring on my finger, put Grits out in the hall, and then take me to that bed over there so we can christen this room properly."

"Yes, ma'am," Wyatt answered with a grin, and covered her mouth with his.

"Oh, and Wyatt?" she whispered against his lips.

"Hmm?"

"Don't forget the blindfold."

—The End—

Thank you for reading WYATT'S STAND. I really hope you enjoyed it and that you'll consider leaving a review at one of your favorite online retailers. It's a great way to help other readers discover new books.

If you liked WYATT'S STAND and would like to read more, turn the page for a list of my other books. And if you don't want to miss any future releases, please join my newsletter:

http://kayleacross.com/v2/newsletter/

Complete Booklist

ROMANTIC SUSPENSE

Colebrook Siblings Trilogy
Brody's Vow
Wyatt's Stand

Hostage Rescue Team Series
Marked
Targeted
Hunted
Disavowed
Avenged
Exposed
Seized
Wanted
Betrayed
Reclaimed

Titanium Security Series
Ignited
Singed
Burned
Extinguished
Rekindled

Bagram Special Ops Series
Deadly Descent
Tactical Strike
Lethal Pursuit
Danger Close
Collateral Damage

Suspense Series
Out of Her League
Cover of Darkness
No Turning Back
Relentless
Absolution

PARANORMAL ROMANCE
Empowered Series
Darkest Caress

HISTORICAL ROMANCE
The Vacant Chair

EROTIC ROMANCE (writing as *Callie Croix*)
Deacon's Touch
Dillon's Claim
No Holds Barred
Touch Me
Let Me In
Covert Seduction

Acknowledgements

A shout out to all my wonderful readers, for supporting this new series.

And as always, a huge thanks to my editing team, cover artist, formatter and DH, for all their help in whipping this baby into shape. It takes a village!

About the Author

NY Times and USA Today Bestselling author Kaylea Cross writes edge-of-your-seat military romantic suspense. Her work has won many awards and has been nominated for both the Daphne du Maurier and the National Readers' Choice Awards. A Registered Massage Therapist by trade, Kaylea is also an avid gardener, artist, Civil War buff, Special Ops aficionado, belly dance enthusiast and former nationally-carded softball pitcher. She lives in Vancouver, BC with her husband and family.

You can visit Kaylea at www.kayleacross.com. If you would like to be notified of future releases, please join her newsletter:

http://kayleacross.com/v2/newsletter/